# SECOND CHANCE AT SUNRISE

# SECOND CHANCE AT SUNRISE

*A Novel By*
CATHERINE COFFEY

*Second Chance at Sunrise* is a work of fiction.
Names, characters, places and incidents are the products of the author's imagination or are used fictitiously. Any resemblance to actual events, locales, or persons, living or dead, is entirely coincidental.

Copyright © 2016 by Catherine Coffey
All rights reserved. No part of this book may be used or reproduced in any form, electronic or mechanical, including photocopying, recording, or scanning into any information storage and retrieval system, without written permission from the author except in the case of brief quotation embodied in critical articles and reviews.

Cover design by The Troy Book Makers
Book design by The Troy Book Makers

Printed in the United States of America

The Troy Book Makers • Troy, New York • thetroybookmakers.com

To order additional copies of this title, contact your favorite
local bookstore or visit www.tbmbooks.com

ISBN: 978-1-61468-361-2

FOR MOM AND DAD

# CHAPTER ONE

From what I could see from my tiny window, the night was moonless and starless. The flight would take about seven hours. I settled back in my seat and began to observe my fellow passengers. They were mostly older couples, probably traveling in a group, taking that much awaited dream vacation overseas.

I watched as people around me smiled and talked excitedly and helped each other stuff baggage into the compartments above their seats. There is always a great deal of settling in that occurs when one boards an airplane. Luggage needs to be stowed, carry-on bags tucked away and passengers secured in their seats. And then there is the careful preparation of the distractions, those things that are going to help you get through the flight – headphones, books, crossword puzzles, knitting.

Flight attendants were working their way up and down the aisles bringing a pillow here and a blanket there. I watched an elderly man helping his wife adjust her seat for maximum comfort. He worked patiently and gently and was rewarded with a kiss. Although they had aged it was obvious the love they shared had stood the test of time. I looked away, envious and aching to have again a love like they shared.

I was going abroad to meet my best friend Nora in England, London to be exact. She had arranged a post for me as secretary to the owner of an import-export company. Actually, she had arranged for my escape.

I was fleeing heartbreak and sorrow. My four-year-old son and my husband of ten years had been killed in a car accident and my world had come to a complete end. My husband and I were only children and we had already buried both sets of parents. Immediately after the car accident Nora Blaisedale came to my side.

She had dropped everything to orchestrate the funeral, the settling of my husband's estate, the sale of his business, the closing of my home. I could not bear to set foot into the house I had shared with my family. Nora arranged for the entire household – furnishings and personal possessions – to be placed in storage and she had listed the house with a realtor. She hadn't stopped there. Since she owned an international employment agency, she had arranged for a job. I was hesitant about leaving the States but she had insisted that the complete change of venue would help me heal. Nora and I had been best friends since college – I trusted her like a sister. Anyway, I was too numb to argue.

And so, just three months after my world had come crashing down, I was traveling to England to begin a new life. Nora had returned ahead of me because of pressing business. It was decided that I would follow alone. Alone…how I hated and feared the very word. I had never been alone in all of my thirty-four years.

True, I had been an only child but my parents and I were extremely close and growing up I had a large circle of friends. And then there was Jack – we had met during our senior year in college, had dated a couple of years and had married. We were good friends, partners and lovers. Of course we had differences as well as similarities, but one seemed to compliment the other. Our relationship became stronger after the death of our parents and stronger yet after Alex's birth.

I could feel the tears welling up inside me and I forced myself to focus on the attendant as she began taking drink orders from the passengers. I was trying not to let another wave of total despair wash over me, but the loss of my husband and child had left such a horrific void in my life there were days when I believed I couldn't go on. Going to live with Nora was the one ray of light left in my life. We had met during our sophomore year at Loyola. She (and Jack, whom I would meet later) was a political science major and I was a student of the communication school but we were housed in the same dorm and introduced by a mutual friend. She and I had become instant friends. Sometimes it's just like that with two people.

Nora had a younger sister who tragically died at the age of eight in a hit and run accident. I sometimes felt, although I never said it out loud, that I had filled the void left by the sibling taken too early. Although we were the same age, it was like she was the older sister. She was more confident, more outspoken and more worldly and she never hesitated to act that way. It didn't matter to me; I let her play the role. I was just thrilled to have her as a friend and confidant. We took some classes together and did a great deal of socializing together.

We had remained close friends, even after graduation as life took us in separate directions, with frequent visits and countless phone calls. Now, she was the only family I had left to cling to. And so I had packed up, picked up and boldly decided to go and start over.

The flight passed without incident. The plane landed at Heathrow. As I made my way through customs, another wave of nausea took me over.

"Are you quite all right, Madame?" my customs officer was saying.

"Yes, yes…I just haven't had a meal in several hours," I said, leaning against the counter for support.

"We're through here, may I call someone for you?"

At that moment I heard Nora's voice above the crowd.

"Ashleigh, Ashleigh darling!" she was calling out and waving.

"Oh, thank you for your concern," I said to the officer, "There's my friend now."

Nora and I exchanged a warm greeting.

"Leigh dear, you look positively exhausted. Here, let me take your bag. We're this way," she said, conducting me through a maze of people and baggage.

She chatted about the weather, the people, the airport and life in general as we made our way outside. Suddenly she stopped.

"Well, here we are. Charles, there is just the one bag," said Nora, handing my luggage over to an impeccably dressed chauffeur. I put him somewhere in his mid to late fifties. He was tall and thin and had beautiful silver hair and mustache to match. Nora had insisted that I travel lightly, promising that she would pick out some new clothes and have them waiting for me. And of course, she had added, we would go shopping together for whatever I needed. The prospect of a new wardrobe and a shopping excursion had sounded good to me and so I had agreed.

"Yes Miss Blaisedale," the man said with a slight bow of the head. He took my bag and headed for the baggage compartment. The limousine was as magnificent as its driver.

"Nora," I said somewhat shocked, "I know you're excited but this is a bit much, isn't it?"

"Darling, this isn't my doing," she answered, "This is compliments of your new employer, Mr. Bruce Spenceworth. Only the best for you…" she broke off suddenly.

"Leigh, what is it? What's wrong?" she was reaching out to hold me.

"It's nothing," I said taking her arm, "I'm just a bit lightheaded. It's been hours since I've eaten, and I'm feeling, well, a bit overwhelmed."

"Let's get in and relax," she directed, "We've a bit of a drive and I have a great deal to tell you."

With that, Charles escorted us to our seats, took his own behind the wheel and the exquisite automobile set off.

We rode in silence for quite some time. I had an idea that Nora was allowing me time to take in the sights. First the city. It had actually been a life long dream of mine to visit England and I still could hardly believe it would now become my home. I had been fascinated by the country ever since I was a child.

My mother had been born and raised in London. She had met my father one summer while he and a college buddy were back-packing across Europe. They had fallen in love and after he came home to the United States, they continued to call and write to each other. Both sets of parents had convinced themselves that it was just a summer romance that would run its course and burn out. But they had been mistaken and my parents married the summer after my father graduated from law school. They settled down in a beautiful Maryland suburb and my father commuted to work in the nation's capitol every day.

My mother never lost her delightful native accent, and she shared many stories and photographs of her childhood with me. She would describe experiences and locations with amazing detail and I would close my eyes and see it as if I'd actually been there. My mother had also been an only child from a small family. I probably had some long lost relatives somewhere in the country but I couldn't imagine how to locate them. I was determined to make a stab at it anyhow once I'd settled in. Anyway, just being in my mother's homeland gave me, oddly enough, a sort of peace.

Now the city was just as I'd imagined it would be and just like all of the pictures I'd ever seen of it. The streets were narrow and lined with charming shops and pubs and markets. History and tradition emanated from every inch of the great city. It was incredible to see Westminster Abbey and Buckingham Palace with my own eyes and St. Paul's Cathedral and Ten Downing Street and the museums. I could hardly wait to walk the streets on a proper tour. They were alive with people and cars and the famous red double-decker buses. I could picture my mother as a child taking the bus here and there to shop and later as an adult with my father on a tour of the city. Our car ventured along many winding lanes revealing seemingly endless sections of the fascinating city until at last, it became apparent we were motoring beyond its limits. We passed picturesque stone-lined fields and houses with thatched roofs. I sat back in my seat allowing the supple leather to envelop me.

"Drink?" Nora asked, finally breaking the silence. She was mixing one for herself at a small bar.

"No thanks," I replied, "I think that alcohol on top of this jet lag would finish me off. Where are we headed by the way? The scenery is magnificent and Charles a superb driver, but I rather thought we'd be heading to my new office or perhaps your flat so I can get settled in."

"Oh no, darling," answered Nora, "We're on our way to meet Bruce and get you settled into your new home."

"Oh," I said somewhat confused and definitely disappointed, "I assumed I'd be staying with you for awhile. Will I at least be staying nearby?"

Just then the car veered off the lane. It was headed down a long, tree-lined driveway. A growing sense of uneasiness crept over me.

"Nora, just what is going on here? Where are we?" I demanded.

Nora grinned and said, "Brookside, the Spenceworth estate."

The words were no sooner spoken when the house came into view. No, not house, huge stately mansion. Before me stood a vast three story stone structure set atop a gradually inclining slope. It was vintage Tudor with a perfectly proportioned 'E' shape and complete with gables topped with gargoyles, scores of mullioned windows and multiple chimneys. Flush with the ground was a massive wooden entry door set dead center of the building and slightly recessed into a stone alcove.

In several spots ivy was growing up the stone walls, in most cases reaching the third story. The building was made of mere stone, plaster and wood but it was the essence of solid serenity. And there was undeniably a harmony between the building and its natural surroundings. It was almost as if they were one. The driveway formed a perpendicular line with the house and became circular near the front door. To the left of the great house were perfectly manicured gardens; to the right, at the foot of the slope, a river. There were no other houses in sight and I wondered how close the nearest neighbor was.

The car came to rest opposite the front door. Charles helped us disembark and then fetched my bag from the trunk.

"Oh, I won't be needing that now," I said.

A strange look passed between Charles and Nora.

"Wait one moment," I said looking from one to the other, "I'm not staying here?"

They were spared from answering my question as just then, the massive front door swung open. A very handsome man and a beautiful young boy stepped forward to greet me.

"Mrs. Grant," the man began, "I am Bruce Spenceworth. May I present my son, Robert. We are so pleased to…"

He was talking and extending his hand. The sight of father and son was too much. Everything went black.

# CHAPTER TWO

**I opened my** eyes and sat up. I was sitting on a massive four-poster bed. As my eyes traveled around the room, I got the impression that I was in a medieval bedchamber. The walls were paneled with dark wood and adorned with tapestries and at least half a dozen antiquated weapons. Here and there hung the taxidermied animal heads from some ancient hunting party. The room contained many pieces of furniture and a fireplace with an ornately carved wooden mantel. I could see through the windows that daylight was fading. All at once I remembered the man and the boy and that I had fainted. Oh, what must my employer be thinking? Just then, the door opened and Nora came in followed by the boy.

"Hey, you're looking better," she said, smiling.

"I'm so sorry Nora," I apologized frantically, "I passed out didn't I? How did I get here?"

"No need for sorry, yes you did and Bruce carried you. Good thing you don't weigh much, love," laughed Nora. Her voice became serious. "Now, Dr. Thompson is just outside. We'll clear out so he can get to work."

"Doctor! Is that really necessary?" I asked in protest.

"Bruce insisted," answered Nora, "And I must say, I agree wholeheartedly. You haven't seemed yourself since I picked you up."

"Very well," I sighed wearily. The boy had been standing silently beside Nora.

"Robert, how old are you?" I asked.

He promptly responded, "Nine years old Mrs. Grant and my friends call me Rob."

He was so well spoken, his demeanor so man-like it was difficult to believe he was only nine. His attempt to include me in his circle of friends warmed my heart.

"Well, Rob," I said, "I hope I didn't give you and your father too much of a fright. I'm all right, really. And my friends call me Leigh."

He gave me a smile and said, "I'll go and fetch Dr. Thompson now Leigh."

"Thank you Rob," I called after him. To Nora I confided, "I'm so embarrassed. Mr. Spenceworth must think I'm…"

I broke off as Dr. Thompson entered the room. Nora silently nodded to the man as she took her leave. The doctor seemed a kindly old man. His hair was white and he wore gold-rimmed glasses with lenses so tiny I wondered why he bothered to wear them at all. His suit jacket seemed somewhat worn and the vest underneath it had definitely seen better days. A stethoscope hung around his neck. He slowly retrieved a chair, placed it beside the bed and sat down. He took a notebook from a medical bag that looked like it belonged in a museum, inquired about my medical history and carefully recorded my answers. He then performed a fairly thorough examination.

"Mrs. Grant," he began, "All appears in order. I would, however, like to conduct one additional test in my office. As it's getting late perhaps you could come round first thing in the morning. For tonight, you are to have a nourishing meal and plenty of sleep."

"I'm not sure how or where…" I started.

As if reading my mind he said, "I'll arrange to have Charles bring you – he knows the way. Put your mind at ease. Goodnight," he said making his way to the door.

"Goodnight, and thank you Dr. Thompson," I called.

The door had barely shut behind him when it flung open again to admit Nora.

"Well?" she asked eagerly.

"Well, I'm fine," I answered somewhat defensively, "I'm just exhausted." I decided not to mention tomorrow's appointment.

"Can you come down to supper? They are rather formal here, or shall I have a tray sent up?" Nora asked.

She certainly sounded like the lady of the manor. All at once I wondered just what kind of relationship existed between her and Mr. Spenceworth. I had never heard her mention his name in a romantic way, but come to think of it, I was in the dark about the current status of her love life. Perhaps theirs was more than a mere business relationship. I didn't have the strength to ask that question.

"I'll come down. Formal dinner is the least I can do after spoiling the introductions. Do I have time to freshen up?" I asked.

"I'm afraid our presence is required now," she replied, "Anyhow, all things considered, you and that pantsuit still look remarkably beautiful."

I smiled appreciatively at the compliment and followed her toward the door. I could hardly wait to see what lay beyond it.

# CHAPTER THREE

Since I had been unable to study my surroundings on the trip upstairs, I gave them considerable scrutiny on the trip down. Beyond my bedchamber stretched a great hallway lined with windows and doors, no doubt bedrooms as well. The floor was made of wood and bits of it were carpeted with several large area rugs. They were worn in spots and I wondered just how old they, and the house, actually were. The walls appeared to be plaster and stone with wood trim, from which hung paintings, probably of family members, and colorful tapestries.

Midway along the hall was a set of double wooden doors guarded on either side by suits of armor – the master bedroom I presumed. Directly across the hall from this were paned glass doors leading onto a large, stone balcony that jutted out from the house. We paused to take in the view. Perfectly manicured gardens and lush lawn continued on as far as the eye could see. The garden looked like a maze from our vantage point – trees and shrubs lined its border, while hedges and flowers were key components of the interior design. At its center stood a large fountain. A stone walk wound its way throughout. I could see several outbuildings, a small church and a cemetery on the immediate grounds and beyond this lay what appeared to be endless miles of fields and forest. A glimpse of the river was also possible.

"Tonight before bed we'll stroll out on the balcony," Nora suggested. "The view of the gardens and the river in the moonlight is breathtaking from up here."

"We'll be staying the night then?" I asked.

She nodded. Again she had demonstrated a certain familiarity toward house and owner. We moved on. At the end of the hall lay the most spectacular staircase I had ever seen. It was made from marble - white marble tread with green marble for the risers and an intricately carved banister of dark wood running up and down both sides. Here one had to make a choice as to whether to ascend another flight or descend, presumably to the first level.

"What is upstairs?" I inquired.

"Oh, the third floor houses the servants' quarters and the nursery and additional bedrooms," Nora replied. "It isn't often used these days, only when the house is full of guests on special occasions."

We began our descent but paused on the landing. One could not miss the life size portrait of a very beautiful woman hanging on the wall.

"Mrs. Spenceworth," said Nora. I stared at the portrait which must have been at least five feet in length and mounted in an enormous gilded golden frame. The woman was incredibly attractive. Her long wavy hair was a dark auburn color and her eyes were sky blue. She was wearing a peacock blue riding suit and was posed on a bench near a fountain, possibly in the garden behind the house. The pose was head-on and the picture pulled me in. It portrayed her beauty but somehow it seemed as though the very essence of her being came alive, almost jumping off the canvass.

I felt a tug at my sleeve and I reluctantly turned away from the portrait. We resumed our downward trek. I was certainly curious about the relationship dynamics in the household, but remained silent. We were met at the bottom of the stairs by Charles and I found myself wondering when the magnificent Mrs. Spenceworth would make her appearance.

"Dinner is served," he announced, and he led the way across the enormous foyer toward a set of wood paneled double doors. Charles grasped both doorknobs and threw back the great doors. He stepped aside, allowing us to make our entrance.

"Ms. Nora Blaisedale and Mrs. Ashleigh Grant," he said ceremoniously. As we advanced further into the room my eyes went immediately to the dining table. It had to be fifteen feet long and was made of a dark wood. It was not covered with a tablecloth therefore showing off its thick legs with claw-like feet. At each place setting there was a lace mat, topped with fine china and crystal and silverware. Large pewter candelabras sat at each end of the table and the largest floral arrangement I'd ever seen sat in the center. The crystal vase alone had to stand two feet from rim to bottom. Shooting up out of the vase were orange and yellow tiger lilies, white long stem roses, cattails, baby's breath and assorted greens. I had never seen that combination of flowers before and it was stunning.

On one wall of the room stood a sideboard so long it ran almost the length of the wall. It held several serving dishes on warmers, carafes of wine and assorted bottles of liquor. Above the sideboard hung a large mirror. Another wall contained a fireplace – one so big a man could fit inside it. The mantel was marble and above it also hung a mirror. It struck me that the use of mirrors in the room gave the impression of the room being even wider and longer than it was. A fire had been laid on so the formality of the room was lessened some.

I began to study my dinner companions. Several men, Rob and of course, Mr. Spenceworth. He had risen, as had the others, at Charles' announcement of our arrival. I was delighted to see that I was being seated next to Rob. I felt that we had become instant friends. Nora had taken the seat opposite Mr. Spenceworth – customarily the one meant for the woman of the house. I wondered again where Mrs. Spenceworth was. Before we were seated, Mr. Spenceworth made the introductions.

"Mrs. Grant," he said, "May I present my attorney Patrick Fergueson, my accountant Edward Stewart and our store's manager Marco Abruzzi." The attorney was a man in his late fifties. He was tall with very dark hair, such dark hair that I thought it was perhaps touched up. He was very well dressed and seemed quite relaxed. The accountant seemed late forties, maybe older, although I couldn't help but notice he seemed to be in excellent shape and I concluded that I might not have gauged an accurate age reading due to his slightly balding salt and pepper hair and his glasses. In contrast to the lawyer, he seemed somewhat anxious but was clearly trying to appear relaxed. The store manager was clearly the youngest of the men and was immaculately dressed. Although he was fair-haired, his skin was dark and his teeth seemed unnaturally white when he smiled. I took an instant, although unexplainable, disliking to the store manager. He reminded me of a predator – silent, still and ready to devour its prey. We exchanged how-do-you-dos and brief pleasantries and then prepared for dinner.

Charles, obviously a very versatile fellow, came in and began serving with dishes from the sideboard. He was followed by a woman I would later come to know as Elizabeth Major. They served our food and drink and periodically reappeared to assess and fulfill our needs or clear away. The food was excellent and I ate rather ravenously. The men mostly talked about business and amongst themselves. Nora would interject from time to time with a lighthearted comment. Her flirtatious, easy-going manner was one of her great assets. She certainly knew how to work a crowd. I smiled a great deal and made light conversation with Rob. I was too tired to attempt anything else.

At one point during the meal, Marco Abruzzi rose and excused himself saying he needed to use the telephone. I couldn't put my finger on why but for some reason Mr. Abruzzi's presence definitely caused me a sense of uneasiness. I thought it strange that I would take such an instant dislike to someone I'd only just met but I couldn't shake the feeling. The dining room door had barely closed when the accountant, Mr. Stewart, also excused himself.

Marco reappeared eventually saying he would have to go, citing business details that required his immediate attention. He shook hands with Bruce and then to my surprise he approached me taking my hand and bowing as he said goodnight. The touch of his hand repulsed me but I forced a smile. Mr. Stewart reappeared as Marco took his leave. I noticed that the men barely acknowledged each other as they passed one another but I put it down to rivalry among coworkers or Marco's haste to leave.

At the conclusion of the meal, Mr. Spenceworth led the way to his study for coffee and dessert. Mr. Stewart announced he would be unable to stay for coffee and made his goodbyes. It was quite possibly my overtired imagination at work but it seemed to me that his goodbye to Nora took longer than anyone else.

Our thinning group made its way toward the study, which was located on the first floor and off the main foyer near the foot of the great staircase. The study was a vast chamber with an undeniably masculine air. It boasted another gigantic fireplace with an intricately detailed mantel made of stone, twin leather couches and a massive walnut desk containing papers, folders, books, a large desk lamp and a telephone. The room also served as a library. Two walls contained floor-to-ceiling built in shelves filled with books. There was even an attached ladder on a track system so that one could reach the uppermost shelves. The very top shelf had been reserved for an impressive duck decoy collection. The carvings were of various sizes and shapes and some were painted while others were just the color of the wood they had been made from.

Coffee and dessert had been laid upon the table between the couches. We were left to serve ourselves. Although the evening had been a pleasant one, I suddenly felt an overwhelming need to retire to my room. I made my apologies, bade everyone goodnight and departed. I had only climbed a few steps when I heard Mr. Spenceworth's voice behind me.

"Mrs. Grant, may I have a word?" he asked quietly.

I turned around. "Of course," I said, making my way back down the stairs. As I stood facing him I realized how tall he was. He had broad shoulders and a fine figure. His hair was dark and he, like Charles, had a mustache. I guessed his age at late thirties or very early forties. He was very handsome indeed. I felt slightly nervous standing there alone with him and it suddenly struck me that there was only one other man that had caused such a reaction within me and that was my husband. I was startled and chided myself for thinking such thoughts.

"I trust that today has not been too much for you," he began, "I should like to spend some time with you tomorrow after your appointment with Dr. Thompson."

So, he had already been told about the doctor's request to see me.

"I'm sorry to be…" I started, but he cut me off.

"Please, no apology is necessary. Charles will take you round first thing and I will see you upon your return. I will send Mrs. Major up now to draw your bath and if there is anything you need please let us know."

I hardly knew what to say. I merely said 'thank you' and headed back up the great staircase. Before entering the long hallway, I paused to look back down toward the foyer as I could feel his eyes watching me. He was still standing there, looking up at me. I forced a smile and then quickly stepped out of his sight. I wondered what he could be thinking.

As I passed the doors to the balcony, I noticed that the moon had risen and its light was shining over the garden and the river. It was as Nora had described – breathtaking. I opened the doors and stepped out onto the balcony. The evening air was chilly but I didn't mind. Table and chairs were present but I walked right to the edge and stood leaning against the stone railing. My thoughts were about my host. Where was Mrs. Spenceworth? Just how much had Nora told him about me? We had only just met and it felt like there was some connection between us. Suddenly I felt homesick and afraid. Those feelings gave way to misery and despair as I remembered I no longer had home or family to return to. I was startled by a sound behind me. I whirled around to find Elizabeth Major standing there.

"I am sorry to frighten you, Mrs. Grant," she said meekly, "I only came to say your bath is drawn and I've seen to your room. From your door, the loo is just down to the right – second door. If there's nothing else…."

I was amazed by the degree of hospitality being showered upon me. I had certainly never experienced anything like it.

"Oh…I…no. There is nothing else. And, thank you Mrs. Major."

She gave me a nod, a slight curtsey and then took herself away as silently as she had come. Although it was hard to tear myself away from the beauty and tranquility of the scene that lay before me, I left the balcony and hastened to my room. The fire in the fireplace was still burning, the cover on my bed was turned back and a lovely dressing gown lay at the foot of the bed. It hadn't come from my bag – I wondered to whom it belonged. Nora? Mrs. Spenceworth? I picked it up and headed for the bathroom. The room proved to be as grand as the rest of the house. A plush carpet covered the floor. The vanity contained his and hers sinks. There was a shower stall, the doors to which were stained glass, and a raised marble tub. The latter was filled with hot bubbly water and looked so inviting. I disrobed and climbed the steps necessary to gain access.

The hot water felt so good. As I relaxed, my mind began replaying the day's events – seeing Nora, arriving at Brookside, meeting Bruce and Rob Spenceworth. Less than twenty-four hours earlier I had been making final preparations for my journey and readying myself to say goodbye to my birthplace and home. I choked back tears as my mind ran a silent picture show spanning the years – the good times, the trying times, the times with my husband and child. I sobbed bitterly, trying to shut the memories out.

As I wiped the tears away, I exited the tub thinking that Nora had been right. I was better off leaving the States and making a fresh start. Leaving meant I wouldn't have to see the house I grew up in, or the park where Jack had proposed or Alex's favorite teddy bear. I could block out the pain by removing myself and I was determined to block out the pain. I redressed, tidied up and headed for my room. I climbed into bed and was asleep as soon as my head hit the pillow.

# CHAPTER FOUR

I'VE NEVER BEEN good at sleeping through the night in a strange place. True to form, I awoke in the wee hours of the morning. The house was silent. I slipped out of bed, opened the door and headed out into the hallway. I was eager for another glimpse out the balcony doors. The moon was darting in and out of the clouds casting an eerie, yet fascinating light on the grounds. I don't know how long I stood gazing out the doors. I was mesmerized by watching the trees bending gently in the breeze and could not stop staring at how the moon's light illuminated the garden below. Here and there a moon ray would cause the river's rushing water to sparkle like a diamond. The sight had a much needed calming affect on my senses. Eventually as I moved to return to my room I saw Mr. Spenceworth. He was clad only in pajama bottoms and was standing in the doorway directly across from the balcony doors, the one with suits of armor on either side. My hunch that the room was the master bedroom had been correct. We stood silently staring at one another. For the second time that night, I forced a smile then hurried away down the hall and climbed back into bed.

I awoke to the sound of someone knocking at my door. Daylight flooded the room.

"Mrs. Grant?" It was Charles.

"Yes?" I called through the door.

"I can have the car ready in twenty minutes. Will that be time enough for you?" he inquired.

"Yes, plenty," I answered, "Thank you, Charles." I hastily made the bed, threw on a skirt and sweater, ran a brush through my long hair and applied some lipstick. On the dressing table I found a note from Nora. *Leigh, left early for appointment. Didn't want to wake you as you sleeping soundly. See you this afternoon. Love N.* She was such a dear friend. I was curious, however, about where she had spent the night. I encountered no one on my trip downstairs. Charles had the car waiting just outside the front door. He saw me to my seat, took his own and we set off.

"Is Dr. Thompson's place far?" I asked.

"No Madame," he replied.

And that was the extent of the conversation between us. The remainder of the short journey passed in silence. I couldn't speak for Charles' but mine was due to intense preoccupation. My mind was reviewing everything from the previous evening's events to where I would be residing, to just why the doctor wanted to see me. In no time we reached the office. It was attached to the house, which was charming. Not too large and made of stone and topped with a thatched roof. A fence covered with wild roses ran the length of the front yard. I could see several outbuildings and animals beyond the main house. There were two entryways and I headed for the one with the sign above the door reading, 'Ian Thompson, MD'. A bell announced my presence as I opened the door and went in. I was surprised to see a middle-aged woman dressed in white coming down the hallway to greet me.

"Morning dear," she said pleasantly. As she came closer I noticed the nametag pinned to her uniform. It read *Mildred Thompson*. How charming, I thought, a husband and wife team. She caught my stare.

"Mrs. Mildred Thompson, but please, do call me Millie. Everyone does," she begged.

I smiled in spite of myself. She seemed so kind. She was holding a newspaper in one hand and a paper cup in the other.

"At it again last night, they were," she said. Then, in answer to the look of confusion on my face, she continued, "Why, the 'London Creeper'. Been robbing precious jewels and artwork from the folks in London and hereabouts being that we're a mere stone's throw away. Clever fellow, that. Once the items have been taken they're never seen here again. Scotland Yard's a wreck. Can't…oh, go on Millie. I do so," she laughed. She handed me the paper cup.

"He'll be needing a sample, my dear," she continued, "The w.c. is just beyond the examination room, there. When you're set, meet me right back here."

I did what she had directed, all the while reflecting on London's 'Creeper'. She led me to the examination room saying the doctor would be with me momentarily. I was beginning to feel butterflies in my stomach, as if I were a student waiting to see the principal. I paced back and forth and then sat down and then repeated this process several times before the doctor entered the room and took the seat opposite mine.

"Mrs. Grant," he began, "I understand you have recently been widowed."

The butterflies were giving way to nausea.

"I hope this won't come as too much of a shock," he continued, "You are with child. I should put it at about twelve weeks from the information you provided last night and your test results just now. I will order a sonogram be performed to confirm."

His words were earth shattering. I could feel my whole body beginning to tremble. A child. Jack's child. It would never know its father or its brother.

"My dear…" the doctor was saying.

Tears were rolling down my face. "Are you…you are…certain?" I sobbed.

"Yes, quite," he replied. He took my hands. "We, all of us, will be here for you whatever decisions you make. Clearly you have had a shock. I'm ordering Charles to take you straight home. You are to have a few days rest and I'll call on you Friday morning. We'll talk again then."

I was sobbing uncontrollably. The doctor helped me to my feet and walked me to the door. Charles and Mildred were waiting on the other side. Mildred gave me a warm embrace and then gently handed me over to Charles, who put an arm around me and guided me, half carrying me, to the car. The return trip was a blur. My heart ached so badly I thought it would burst from my chest. I could not stop crying and thought I should go mad from grief. We were headed along the drive when I ordered Charles to stop the car.

"I beg your pardon, Mrs. Grant?" he said.

"Stop this car!" I demanded through my tears, "Please stop it at once."

Immediately the vehicle came to a halt. Charles came around and opened my door. I stepped out and started running. Charles made no attempt to call after me or to stop me. I went through the trees lining the drive and out into an open field. I ran as if running could stop the pain. I had grieved when Jack and Alex died. But now I was doing it all over again and this time, the pain was ten-fold. I tripped on something, a rock I think and fell to my knees but got up and started running again. The sound of a galloping horse behind me made me slow down and look behind me. The rider was Mr. Spenceworth. He was dismounting even before his horse had come to a full stop. I came to a standstill and slowly sank to my knees. He was running toward me and very quickly reached me, kneeling down to face me. He was a total stranger to me and yet in a moment he had taken me into his arms. It felt so good, so safe to have his arms around me. I cried without hesitation; he held me without saying a word.

I've no idea how long we knelt there in our embrace. All at once I began to feel extremely self-conscious. He sensed my sudden tenseness.

"Ashleigh…" he began.

"Mr. Spenceworth," I interrupted, and as I broke free from his arms, I stood up. "I apologize…I…it's just that I…I've had a bit of a shock…" I was stumbling badly, making a complete fool of myself.

"Ashleigh," he said again standing up, "Please come with me." He extended his hand.

I looked into his eyes. There was…something… behind his intense gaze. I felt some kind of instant connection with him. I took his hand and together we retrieved his horse. He helped me into the saddle and then seated himself behind me. He reached forward and grabbed the reigns. Once again his arms encircled me. I was so scared and so alone that I allowed myself to take comfort in his closeness. This time I was acutely aware of an electrifying sensation when we touched. We rode to a clearing behind the house near the river. He dismounted and then gently lifted me to the ground. There was a bench near the water. He led me to it and we sat down. Although we sat in silence for some time, I had the feeling that he wanted to say something. I wondered why he didn't. Finally, unable to bear the silence, uncertain about what he wanted and overwrought with emotions, I blurted out, "I…I'm…Dr. Thompson says I am going to have a baby. I should have known. I can't believe this is happening…..I can't believe my family is gone…" I was weeping uncontrollably again. He was sitting close enough to put his arm around me and he did.

"I know. Dr. Thompson rang the house. I was coming to meet the car. Ashleigh, there is so much I want to say to you," he said, "I hardly know where to begin. First, I want you to rest assured you are not alone. You will stay here with Rob and myself. Brookside will be your home."

"You have been most generous," I managed, "But I am a total stranger. I could not possibly impose on you and Mrs. Spenceworth. My problems…"

"Mrs. Spenceworth has been dead these nine years," he interrupted, "She died giving birth to Rob."

"Oh…Oh, I'm so sorry," I apologized, "I didn't know."

"Quite all right," he said, "Rob and I have done well for ourselves."

"Yes," I agreed, wiping my face and choking back more tears, "Rob is a remarkable boy, and he seems very happy."

"He is everything to me," he said, and then he changed the subject, "And you are hardly a stranger. Nora has spoken of you so often over the years that I feel as if I know you."

"Nora talks about me?" I asked fumbling in my pocket for a tissue.

"Please, allow me," he said offering his handkerchief, "She is really quite fond of you and frequently spoke about your husband's investigation firm and your journalistic capabilities over the years."

"Really, she must have bored you," I said, embarrassed, "Private investigation and journalism are a far cry from the import-export business."

"On the contrary," he said, "And mystery is a –er- hobby of mine. I've read several of the papers you've published."

I was flattered that he knew of my work. I had written articles on a variety of subjects and many about Jack's most notable cases. He had started out small but was soon receiving work from many prestigious law firms, my father's included. The FBI had even hired him to assist on several cases. Jack had taken his business from a one-man show to a company employing thirty people. I had been so proud of him. After his death several of the investigators he had employed approached Nora about buying the firm. I had been glad that the company would remain in the hands of people Jack had worked with and trusted.

Morning had given way to early afternoon. It was a lovely day. There was a soft breeze blowing; it felt so refreshing. And the sound of the water running by was so soothing. I wasn't sure how to respond to the invitation to stay at Brookside, so I said, "Mrs.

Thompson mentioned that London has fallen prey to a 'Creeper'."

"Yes," he replied, "A clever thief. The bloke is certainly giving the authorities the dickens of a time."

"'Creeper'?" I asked.

"A bit unusual, but nevertheless appropriate. Apparently several of the burglaries have occurred while the family was on the premises," he offered.

That thought sent a chill down my spine. Broaching new territory I said, "Tell me about the job I'm to fill. Nora says you need a secretary. Of course I know nothing about the import-export business, but I'm a quick study and I…"

"I do need a secretary," he interjected, "However, I would like to make a proposal." He was sitting there facing me with such an intense look about him, I began to feel nervous. "Would you do me the honor of becoming my wife?"

It was quite literally a proposal. I felt very hot and could feel the blush spreading across my face. I was speechless.

"Clearly I have astounded you," he said, undaunted by my reaction. "Please, I am in earnest. Rob and I would be honored. And I would give the baby the Spenceworth name…"

"Why?" I interrupted, "Why would you do this? You don't even know me. And what of you and Nora?" I hadn't meant to ask so bluntly about their relationship, but it just slipped out.

He laughed. "Nora and I are dear friends. We have been for quite some time and will remain so, I expect," he answered. He was so handsome and confident and overwhelming. Words came so easily for him. And he apparently had an agenda, which unbelievably, included me.

"But you are wealthy. There must be any number of women in your own circle…" I started.

"I realize this is sudden and unexpected," he remarked, "However, I know in time you will come to see this union will be right for both of us. Please trust me."

My brain was on overload. This had certainly been one hell of a morning. He sensed my confusion.

"Come," he said, standing up. "Let me show you Brookside." He reached for my hand. I hesitated only a moment, then took his. Again he helped me into the saddle and then took his place behind me. I was afraid to admit to myself just how much I liked the feeling of having him close to me. A slow trot brought us back toward the house. On the way he pointed out the stables and the family chapel and cemetery.

"My family has been in residence here for three hundred years," he said proudly.

"Have you always had such magnificent gardens?" I asked.

"No," he replied, "My great, great grandfather's second wife had a passion for flowers. It was she who developed and implemented the plan to transform the grounds into what you now see. Prior to that the land had been used for grazing, as farming was the family's main source of income. And it was my great, great grandfather's extraordinary head for business that gave rise to the trade company that now bears our name. We have offices in London and Edinburgh."

"What of the rest of your family?" I inquired, "Do you and Rob live in that huge house by yourselves?"

"My parents were killed in a boating accident just under two years ago," he said abruptly, "I am an only child. There are numerous relatives about – aunts, uncles, cousins and the like. And we certainly are not alone. We share the house with two gardeners, one cook, one chambermaid, a stableman, Charles and Mrs. Major."

We were close to the house now and it was nearly lunchtime. It had been almost magical being alone with him. I didn't want the feeling to end, but it did as Charles came to greet us.

"Mr. Spenceworth," he said, "There is an urgent call."

We dismounted and Mr. Spenceworth excused himself and went on ahead of me into the house.

"Charles," I said somewhat shyly, "I want to thank you for taking such good care of me this morning."

"Of course, Madame," he replied. No questions or comments, just one hundred percent manners our Charles. He took the horse and disappeared around the side of the house. I entered the foyer and was warmly greeted by Rob and Nora.

"Are you all right?" Nora inquired, as she came to me and took me in her arms.

"I will be," I answered, hugging her and summoning up as much false bravado as I could.

She broke our embrace and held me at arms length as she stared intently at me, as though trying to get the real read on my state of mind. She knew me only too well and I hoped that my acting job would hold up under the intense inspection.

"Ready for lunch Leigh?" Rob asked.

"I'm famished," I said smiling, glad for the interruption.

Nora and I followed Rob through a door at the rear of the foyer. It led out into a hallway, which according to Rob, led to "the kitchen, the breakfast room, the conservatory and the ballroom". As we made our way I said to Nora, "Now I understand the true nature of your business."

"What do you mean?" she demanded sharply.

"Matchmaking," I replied dryly. She looked somewhat startled. It was a pleasure to see her in the hot seat for a change. We had reached the breakfast room – a bright, cheery and cozy room, which overlooked the gardens. We seated ourselves.

"Oh," Nora said with a nervous laugh. For the first time since I'd known her, she actually seemed at a loss for words. "Well, I…." She was spared further explanation as the door swung open and Mr. Spenceworth appeared. He smiled at Nora, gave Rob a hug and asked to see me for a moment, alone. My heart started pounding so loudly I thought the others would hear it. We stepped out into the hallway.

"There is a situation I must attend to at the office. I would like to dine alone with you this evening… to continue the conversation we were having earlier," he finished. He almost seemed slightly flustered, a condition I hadn't thus far seen him in.

My whole body felt hot.

"I've made special plans," he continued, "Charles will help you be ready. Please, say you will join me?"

He took my hand and raised it toward his lips. I felt myself draw in a breath and hold it. Although he stopped just short of his lips, I still felt a shudder of excitement and anticipation engulf me. He looked me straight in the eye. I nodded my head.

"Until tonight then," he said, and then he was gone.

I stood alone in the hallway wondering just what on Earth was happening to me. And what on Earth was happening between me and Bruce Spenceworth? Life suddenly did not seem real. Somewhat dazed I re-entered the room and immediately encountered two pair of inquisitive eyes. Neither party spoke however, and I found myself deeply appreciative of their silence. Obviously they were curious but, I told myself, here was a show of good manners. No questions, just respect for one's privacy. As I made my way to my seat I caught a glimpse of my reflection in the mirror above the sideboard. Obviously they needn't have asked anything – the telltale blush on my face revealed it all. I took my seat. Brunch had been served in my absence.

"This looks delicious," I said as I began to serve myself. My comment seemed to give the others permission to speak once again. We enjoyed some light-hearted conversation with our meal. Then Charles and Mrs. Major cleared away and served coffee.

"Robert, it is time for your music lesson," Charles reminded the boy.

"Yes, Charles," said Rob obediently. To me he said, "Will you join me for tea?"

"I'd be delighted," I answered, "By the way Rob, what instrument are you studying?"

"The piano," he said smiling as he ran from the room.

Nora and I had been friends a very long time and yet, an awkward silence now hung between us. I was uncertain how to tell her about all of the morning's events and about the situation between Mr. Spenceworth and myself.

"So, when is the wedding?" she asked, breaking the silence.

I was shocked, not only about the fact that she already knew about the proposal, but also about the fact she thought I'd accept it.

"You can't be serious!" I said.

"Why not?" she asked.

"Why not? I…we…I've only known the man one day! I've just buried my husband and child… and now I'm going to…I'm going to have a baby. I can't believe I didn't know. I should have known. Things haven't exactly been regular but I put it down to the extreme stress I've been under," I finished, tears rolling down my face.

Nora moved her chair closer to mine and took my hands. "Leigh, I know all that" she began, "Charles told me about the baby. He's no gossip; he is genuinely concerned. You were so upset this morning and when I arrived he thought I should know."

I nodded. I could not manage words.

"Look," she continued, "I've known you, and Bruce, a long time. I would not have introduced you if I wasn't sure about the two of you. You are both at a point in your lives where you need one another."

"Then, this whole thing was premeditated?" I asked angrily, "There was never any job…"

"Leigh," she said calmly, "I know how much you loved Jack and Alex. No one will ever replace them. But look, darling, Jack would be the first one to insist that you didn't spend the rest of your life alone. You know he would. And now there's to be a child. You've got to live and go on. And you should do it with someone who will love you. Bruce is a good man. Love, I have never steered you wrong, you must trust me. Your emotions are too close to the surface for you to see this clearly. Now, or five years from now, Bruce

Spenceworth is right for you," She paused, looking at me, "You can feel it too, can't you?"

"I….I don't know what you mean" I finished weakly, not sure why I was bothering to deny it and knowing that she could see that I was obviously affected by the man.

"Ah-huh," she replied, "Okay, well you will see what I mean."

She was in complete earnest, it was obvious from her tone and the look in her eyes. I remembered how Bruce had been so earnest that morning. It struck me as odd that they were both so insistent that our 'union' should happen. I still couldn't quite accept what she was saying.

"You really believe I should accept the man's proposal?" I asked.

"I do," she said. Then glancing at her watch she said, "Oh, I've got to run and you've got a date to prepare for. I'll see you tomorrow. I thought maybe we could fit a walking tour of London somewhere into your day, if you're feeling up to it."

"Oh that would be wonderful," I said excitedly, "It's a date!"

With a hug and a kiss she took her leave. I sat alone at the table. As her words replayed themselves in my mind I wondered just how she already knew about my date that evening. My thoughts were interrupted by Mrs. Major.

"Begging your pardon, Madame," she said, "But you are to meet Charles out front. He's to take you to the store."

"The store?" I repeated.

"Oh yes. They're to fit your dress for this evening," she answered with a smile.

It seemed that everyone was aware of and eagerly preparing for my date. I thanked her and made my way to the foyer. I opened the door to find Charles standing at attention next to the car. Without a word we took our seats. Unable to resist, I donned a serious voice and commanded, "To the store, Charles!" He smiled, slightly bowed his head and we set off.

# CHAPTER FIVE

THE STORE PROVED to be Harrods of London. The legendary store spanned several city blocks to cover fifteen acres and was like a small city unto itself. Anything one could possibly want could be found inside. Charles commented that I would have to revisit the site at night as the exterior of the building was outlined in thousands of white lights. Once inside, we made our way to the women's formal attire section. Charles gave my name to a clerk and within minutes we were ushered to a private showing room.

We sat side by side as a steady stream of women walked by modeling the most exquisite evening gowns I had ever seen. The selection was amazing and I felt as if I were covering the premiere showing of some famous designer. It was when I turned to look at Charles' reaction to the whole affair that I was reminded that this showing was exclusively for me and I concluded at once that Bruce Spenceworth had made all the arrangements. It was strange and yet exciting that such a fuss would be made over me.

At the show's conclusion, the clerk assisting us

came for my selection. It was hard to choose and in the end the gown I chose was midnight blue in color. Blue had always been one of my favorite colors. The gown's high-necked bodice was covered in a sheer material. It became silk where it met the bustline, which was appliquéd with sequins and was very form fitting. The skirt was long and full and made of silk. Although I was three months pregnant, my figure did not show it. The dress fit beautifully. I was beginning to feel like Cinderella. The gown was to be pressed and sent by courier to Brookside. As we left the room I decided to go all the way.

"Charles," I said, "I should like to have my hair done."

"Certainly, Madame," he replied.

"Charles, could you possibly manage 'Leigh' when we're alone?" I asked.

He hesitated and then smiled. "Of course, Leigh," he agreed.

Charles summoned the concierge who made arrangements for me to visit the hair salon without delay. I wondered just exactly what Charles had said to the man because I was whisked away and given the royal treatment. The stylist swept my long dark hair into a flattering up-do. I glanced at the clock.

"Charles, will we be on time for tea at Brookside?" I inquired, "Rob is expecting me."

"Yes Leigh," he answered, "If we leave at once."

The return trip passed in silence. I sat trying to process the day's events: an unexpected pregnancy, an equally unexpected marriage proposal and an invitation to dine alone with Bruce. Alone with Bruce. I was amazed at how excited, and nervous, I was at the prospect of being alone with him. I found myself struggling to keep hold of good old common sense. My emotions were certainly having a field day.

Upon returning to Brookside I went straight to the drawing room – a sort of formal living room situated off the foyer next to the dining room. Rob was there and Mrs. Major was just bringing in the teacart.

"Wow!" exclaimed Rob, "Your hair looks beautiful!"

"Why, thank you Rob," I said smiling.

It was to be just the two of us. We sat facing one another on matching couches. Tea was laid out on a wooden teacart inlaid with an intricate mother-of-pearl design. I poured. Conversation was usually so easy with us, but now there was an awkward silence as each struggled to find something to say. We sat buttering our scones.

Finally Rob blurted out. "Will you marry my father and be my mother?" His innocence and sincerity touched my heart. My eyes filled with tears.

"Oh no," he cried, "I didn't mean to make you cry."

"You haven't," I assured him, wiping my tears. "You and your father have been nothing but kind and generous since I arrived here. I am honored that you have asked me to join your family. It's just that…I…sometimes I get sad…" I broke off, fighting back tears.

"Oh I know," said Rob, "You miss your family. There is nothing worse than not being with family. I miss my mother, even though I never knew her. And I miss not having any brothers and sisters to play with. What was your little boy like?" He had come around and was now sitting beside me.

"Alex was very bright and so handsome. He loved to go everywhere with me, and he enjoyed helping me make dinner. I used to take him with me wherever I went. I loved seeing the world through his eyes. I miss him so much," I said. The tears were rolling down my cheeks. Rob put one arm around me and was mopping up my tears with the other. Just then, Mr. Spenceworth entered the room.

"Good evening, all. I---what's happened?" he demanded, as he took in the scene.

"It's quite all right," I said, pulling myself together. "Rob and I were talking about some happy memories. I just got myself all worked up." I gave Rob a hug and a kiss.

"Quite right, then," Mr. Spenceworth said. He glanced at his wristwatch. "I believe you have a dinner engagement to prepare for," he said. He and Rob were staring so intently at me I squirmed in my seat.

"I…yes…I'll just be off then," I said making a hasty exit. Outside in the foyer I breathed a sigh of relief. Mrs. Major came toward me.

"There is a telephone call for you," she said, "I was just coming to fetch you."

"For me?" I was surprised, but I accompanied her to the extension outside Bruce's study. She handed me the receiver and then left me alone.

"Hello" I said into the device.

"Go home!" a voice demanded, "You're not safe at Brookside."

"Excuse me?" I answered, unsure that I had heard the caller correctly.

"Leave England at once!" the voice continued. It was definitely a man's voice.

"Who is this?" I demanded but the connection was abruptly terminated. I placed the receiver back in its cradle and stood there mulling over the brief exchange.

Who would make such a call and why should I leave? I concluded that perhaps the caller had reached the wrong number as he had never actually used my name.

Still replaying the call in my mind, I headed upstairs to finish my preparations for the evening. I stopped on the landing beneath Mrs. Spenceworth's portrait. What would she think of my joining her family? What would Jack think? As I stood there it suddenly hit me. I would be marrying into great wealth and tradition. I could not believe I was actually considering the proposal. And yet, I desperately longed to be a part of a family again. And what of my unborn baby? I certainly wanted it to be born into a loving home. Love. It was the one thing missing between myself and Mr. Spenceworth. Perhaps it would come in time. I stared at the portrait. It was so life-like. The artist had certainly captured the very essence of the woman. All at once, the corners of the mouth turned upward forming a smile. Astounded, I took a step backward. I could not believe my eyes and yet, there was Mrs. Spenceworth smiling at me. My heart began pounding and I shut my eyes tightly. I opened them to find that the picture looked as it had before. Obviously fatigue was wrecking havoc on my eyesight. I was so sure I saw – no, it was fatigue. Shaken, I hurried along to my room. My thoughts were interrupted as Mrs. Major was waiting there for me. She was unwrapping my gown.

"You will look stunning in this," she commented.

"Thank you Mrs. Major," I answered.

"Now, what may I do to help you?" she inquired.

I thought for a moment then said, "Do I have time for a quick bath?"

She glanced at the mantel clock, "Yes, certainly. I'll draw it."

After she left I quickly undressed and donned my dressing gown. I headed down the hallway toward the bathroom. Mrs. Major was putting the finishing touches on my bath.

"There now," she said, "I'll leave you to it."

When she had departed I settled in for a soothing soak. I realized with some surprise that I was feeling like a young girl preparing for her first date – giddy and nervous. I was certainly a contradiction in emotions. On one hand I had been devastated by the loss of my family and I had thought I would remain numb to the world for the rest of my life. On the other, I felt a strange comfort living now in my mother's homeland with Nora close, and the prospect of a child and a new family had me on the verge of elation. Maybe there would be a second chance at happiness for me. I didn't linger in the bath and soon made my way back to my room. Mrs. Major was waiting for me.

"I'd be pleased to help you dress, ma'am," she said.

I begged her, as I'd done Charles, to call me 'Leigh'. She agreed. I slipped on the gown and she zipped me up. She stepped back for an evaluation.

"You do look stunning," she exclaimed, "You'll take the master's breath away."

I flushed under such high praise.

"I'll leave you to finish now," she said, "Come to the dining room when you're ready." She headed for the door.

"Thank you Mrs. Major," I called after her. I sat at my vanity primping my hair and making up my face. There was a knock at the door.

"Come in," I called. It was Rob, dressed in his pajamas and carrying a single yellow rose. He came over to where I was sitting.

"For you," he said simply, "Nora says they're your favorite."

"She's right," I said taking the flower. "It's beautiful and you are very thoughtful to bring it." He turned to leave but quickly turned back and ran into my arms. I hugged and kissed him. I rejoiced in the warmth of his little body and the fragrant smell of his freshly shampooed hair. The joy of holding a child again brought me to the verge of tears but I choked them back so Rob would not see them. He gently pulled away, smiled and quietly took his leave. I sat there a moment pulling myself together and savoring the smell of my rose. Again there was a knock at the door.

"Come in," I called again.

The door opened this time to admit Charles carrying a silver tray. As he came nearer I could see that it contained a black velvet box. He came right over to where I was seated and presented the tray.

"Compliments of Mr. Spenceworth," he announced ceremoniously.

I reached for the box with trembling fingers. Beneath the lid lay a sapphire and diamond necklace, with earrings to match.

I gasped. "Oh," I exclaimed, "Oh, they're...I've never seen anything like it. ...." I broke off. There was a note, *'A token of my sincerity – Bruce'*.

Charles set the tray down, took the necklace from its box and clasped it around my neck. He handed me the earrings. Obeying his silent command, I put them on. I sat staring at my reflection.

"You look lovely, Leigh," he commented, "May I escort you down to dinner?"

"Yes, thank you Charles," I said gratefully. I stood

up and took one final look in the mirror. The gown, the hair-do, the jewelry – I felt like a princess. Charles offered his arm. I took it but before we left the room, he showed me how I could secure the jewels later that evening in a wall safe tucked neatly behind one of the hanging tapestries. I wondered what Charles thought about London's daring burglar and just how much of a temptation Brookside might be for the brazen robber. We made our way downstairs to the dining room. As we passed the portrait, I stole a quick glance at Mrs. Spenceworth. All was in order. I felt certain my earlier experience with the picture had been the result of a very trying day. Charles left me standing a few feet from the dining room doors. He opened them and announced my arrival.

"Ashleigh Grant," he said, and I made my entrance. I heard him close the doors behind me. The first thing I noticed was that the main dining table had not been set. Instead, a smaller, more intimate table for two had been set close to the fireplace. And the room was illuminated by the light of scores of candles. I smiled as I imagined Charles and Mrs. Major arduously placing and lighting each one. Mr. Spenceworth had been sitting at the table. He had risen and was coming toward me. He was impeccably dressed in a black tuxedo. He took my hands.

"Leigh, you are a vision. You look stunning," he offered.

I smiled at the compliment and said, "The same can definitely be said of you."

He smiled and led the way to the cozy table. He seated me and then himself. I touched the necklace.

"Mr. Spenceworth…" I started.

"Please," he interrupted, "Please, call me Bruce. It belonged to my mother and hers before her and so on. It is what one might call an heirloom."

"It is exquisite," I said, "But I couldn't possibly…"

"You must," he insisted, "It was my wife's favorite piece."

I gasped.

"Leigh, whatever is it?" he asked.

"It's…it's nothing. It's just that I realize how very precious this is," I answered, trying to cover my anxiety about the fact that it had been Mrs. Spenceworth's favorite. At that moment, I half expected her to burst through the doors and rip it from my neck.

"Well, to continue," Bruce was saying, "Those pieces have been passed among Spenceworth women for nearly two hundred years. Now they belong there around your neck."

I hardly knew what to say. I said, "I shall treasure them." I had taken notice of his reference to the "Spenceworth women" as if he were confident that I was to become one of them.

There was a momentary silence and I was afraid the evening would be full of them. As if looking for a way to break the silence, Bruce rose from the table and headed toward the fireplace, reaching for a poker on his way. While he tended to the fire, I couldn't help but admire how handsome he was. He moved with such grace and confidence, probably the result of an aristocratic upbringing. It suddenly struck me how different from Jack he was. The thought of Jack made my stomach turn. Before I could sink into despair, Bruce had returned to the table and started talking about his company and before I knew it, we were engaged in a lively discussion of its history and its current standing.

It seemed that although it had humble beginnings, business was now being conducted with the far East, several South American countries, European neighbors, the United States and Mexico. And all handled by the London and Edinburgh offices. As we talked, Charles and Mrs. Major had been in and out silently and efficiently serving and clearing dinner. Over coffee, Bruce declared that he wanted me to take an active part in the company by writing various articles about it, which would be published worldwide. I gave my consent eagerly and it was decided that I would accompany him to the office the following morning to get a first hand look at just how business was conducted. I would attend a meeting between Bruce and his department heads and later take a tour of the building. I would also lunch with Nora and start my walking tour of London.

"I realize we have an early call Leigh," he said, "But I'd like you to come with me to the ballroom."

I nodded my head. I had been enjoying the evening so much, and his company, that I did not want to see it end. He helped me from my chair and offered his arm. I took it and we headed for the ballroom. It was a room I had not seen yet. As we approached the door I could hear the beautiful music of a quartet. Charles, ever ready, was at the door to admit us. The room was magnificent. The floor was patterned marble and there were floor-to-ceiling windows on three walls. The ceiling contained a large circular window through which we could see the evening sky. The room was lit by the moon and the stars and several candelabra strategically placed. Soft, romantic music was courtesy of a string quartet neatly tucked in one corner. My senses were on overload. The man was undeniably a master at the fine art of romance.

"Dance with me Leigh," he requested.

I hesitated momentarily. I knew I would like the feeling of being in his arms and yet I was afraid of it. Our eyes met and I found myself wondering what he was thinking. If he was nervous or excited nothing in his demeanor gave it away. I hoped my feelings were hidden as well. I slowly moved toward him. He put his arms around me very gently and at first he did not hold me too tightly. Eventually, as the night wore on, our bodies became pressed together with our faces touching cheek to cheek. We spoke no words then, but it was as if there was communication between us. Inexplicably, I did have feelings for this man whom I had only known for roughly forty-eight hours and for the first time since the loss of my family I felt I could be happy again.

We danced on and on and I did not want the moment to end. Finally, however, Bruce announced we must say goodnight. Hand in hand we left the ballroom, passed through the foyer and climbed the great staircase. I avoided looking at the portrait. I couldn't face the first Mrs. Spenceworth after I'd just danced so intimately with her husband. Instead of seeing me straight to my room, Bruce led me through the glass doors and out onto the balcony. It was a glorious evening, somewhat mild. We stood silently under the moon, taking in the view. Suddenly Bruce turned toward me. He took a small box from his jacket pocket. He opened it and knelt down on one knee.

"Leigh, please marry me," he said.

"Yes Bruce. Yes, I will marry you," I answered. I heard my voice and I heard the words but I could not believe they had come from my mouth. I had wondered what I would actually say if the moment came. It had come, and so had my answer, easily and without reservation. He stood up, took the ring from its box and slipped it onto my finger. I had begun to cry. He gently brushed the tears from my face. My heart began beating wildly from his touch. He pulled me toward him very slowly and kissed me very tenderly on the cheek and then put his arms around me. We stood locked in our embrace for what seemed an eternity. When we separated, he smiled at me and then he guided me to my door and bade me goodnight.

# CHAPTER SIX

THE NEXT MORNING I awoke early. I had slept soundly. The first thing I did was look at my finger. Yes, indeed, there was a ring – the largest pear shaped diamond I had ever seen – sitting on my finger. It had not been a dream. I lay there happily recalling the evening's events. There was a knock at my door. I expected to hear Charles' voice, but was pleasantly surprised to hear Bruce's.

"Good morning Leigh," he called, "Charles will have the car ready in one half hour. Can you manage that?"

"Oh yes," I replied, "I'll see you then."

I sat up in bed and noticed my evening gown. I smiled, again remembering the magical night. I was still somewhat amazed that I'd actually accepted Bruce's proposal. Suddenly I remembered how it had taken years for Jack and me to decide to marry and here I was accepting a proposal from a man I'd known only a matter of days. Perhaps I had become less cautious in my older age. Perhaps I was reacting to my grief. I had searched my mind and could not really produce a reason for not going forward. Bruce and his son were charming and irresistible. With some difficulty I did acknowledge my own selfish motives for wanting to accept Bruce's proposal. I was alone in the world and expecting a baby. I had once been happily married and raising a child. Now I had the incredibly good fortune to be presented with the opportunity to regain what I had lost and even more - something would be wrong with me if I didn't seize this opportunity I told myself.

I forced myself to dress and quickly tidied the room. I noticed the velvet case containing the jewels Bruce had given me. After opening the lid to be sure they were there, I locked them securely in the wall safe as Charles had shown me. Then I headed downstairs. Bruce and Rob were waiting for me in the foyer. Rob rushed into my arms.

"Leigh, I am so happy," he exclaimed. Obviously his father had shared my answer with him.

I had knelt down to meet his embrace. I looked up at Bruce. He was clearly moved by the sight of us.

"I am happy too, Rob," I returned.

"Come along you two," said Bruce. We made our way outdoors to Charles and the car. Bruce explained that we would drop Rob at school on the way to the office. He went on to say that Rob attended a private school for boys. The campus consisted of an elementary school and a college preparatory high school. I smiled as I watched Rob intently reading the morning newspaper as we drove along. He looked like a junior executive.

All at once Rob exclaimed, "The 'Creeper' was at it again last night!"

"Oh no," I said. Bruce took the paper and skimmed the article. Apparently the daring burglar had robbed a home not far from Brookside. We took turns speculating in a light-hearted manner about what sort of person the 'Creeper' must be. Before long we reached the school. After a hug and kiss from Bruce and I, Rob was escorted to the door by Charles. We waited in silence for Charles' return, but Bruce did reach for my hand to hold. Upon Charles' return we made our way to the company offices in London. The building was a huge five-story structure that occupied a full city block on the York Road overlooking the Thames. It stood close to the Waterloo Station and had a nice view of Westminster Abbey. Charles left us at the front door, at which stood a uniformed attendant. The man said 'Good Morning' to Bruce and gave me a slight bow, with cap removed.

"Good Morning, Peter," Bruce replied. It was shortly after nine in the morning but already the establishment was buzzing with business. And as we entered the lobby, Bruce was besieged by several employees – some with greetings and others with pressing business to discuss. He made his way, with me in tow, effortlessly working the crowd. Inquiring glances were cast my way but I merely smiled and remained silent. Bruce was running this show and I presumed he had a plan.

Finally we moved beyond the entry, away from the crowd and after passing along several hallways we now stood before a solitary elevator. It was operated by a single key. Bruce reached inside his shirt collar and removed a chain from around his neck, from which hung said key. Once its work had been done the key was returned to its hiding place. Inside the elevator there was only one button to select, on which appeared the number five. I surmised this must stand for the fifth floor and contain the executive offices. The ride to the top was a quick one. The door opened to reveal a suite of offices very richly decorated. There were several people about and the man I recognized as Marco Abruzzi, the store manager, was coming to greet us.

"Well good morning Mr. Spenceworth, and it is Mrs. Grant, is it not?" he said smiling. He took my hand and made, I thought, an overly ostentatious bow.

"Mr. Abruzzi," I said, acknowledging his greeting. He had taken my left hand and now suddenly had noticed my diamond. He quickly glanced from me to Bruce but asked no questions. Bruce did not acknowledge the inquiring glance and I followed his lead. There was nothing charming about Mr. Abruzzi in my estimation, quite the contrary. I wondered how such a man came to be the store's manager.

As I looked away to study my surroundings, I caught sight of Mr. Stewart and Nora huddled together in the entryway of an office. I started toward them and at once they moved into the office's inner sanctum. By the time I reached the door and peered in, they were engaged in an intimate embrace.

"Oh, please excuse me," I exclaimed, feeling very embarrassed.

Nora threw her head back, her arms still around Mr. Stewart. "Do come in Leigh," she said laughing.

I hesitated only a moment but did what she commanded. I was not sure what to make of the scene.

"Until later, my dear," Mr. Stewart said, bowing and kissing Nora's hand. "Mrs. Grant" he said acknowledging me on his way out. I merely smiled and nodded my head.

Nora continued to laugh. "You needn't look so shocked," she said.

"I'm sorry," I apologized, "I was just taken by surprise. You never said…..I didn't know that you and Mr. Stewart were…..were…." I stumbled for the right word.

"Lovers?" she finished for me.

"Look, if you're happy, then I'm happy," I said. I was guessing that the man was considerably older than Nora but who was I to make any judgment about relationships.

"Look, love, I'll fill you in later," she said, motioning toward Bruce. "He's looking for you."

I followed her glance and saw that Bruce was indeed signaling for me to rejoin him. I gave Nora a quick hug and hurriedly we confirmed our plans to meet for lunch and start our walking tour of London.

As I rejoined Bruce, he was asking Marco, "Have our guests arrived for the breakfast meeting?"

Marco had regained his composure, whatever he had been thinking about my ring.

"Yes, Mr. Spenceworth," he said, "They are assembled in the board room over coffee."

"Fine," remarked Bruce, "I'll fetch my notes and be along straight away. Leigh."

Fortunately he had invited me to follow. I had no desire to be left alone with Marco Abruzzi. Bruce led the way to a set of doors outside of which sat a woman at a desk – the secretary, I presumed.

"Leigh, may I present Lydia Markham," Bruce said, "She has been working as my temporary secretary these past several months. Mrs. Peabody, who'd been in service with us thirty years, retired in May."

"How do you do," I said warmly.

Although she attempted a pleasant greeting she was obviously sizing me up. And it was apparent to me that she did not like what she saw. Bruce had moved into his office. I paused at the doorway and glanced in. The office, like his home office, was reflective of his character – strong, bold pieces of furniture complimented by a conservative color scheme. The building was turn of the century so he even had a fireplace, which added warmth and charm to the room. The phone on Ms. Markham's desk rang. She answered it and then handed the receiver in my direction, advising me that the caller had asked for me. Startled, I took it, wondering who knew I was there.

"Hello," I said.

"There is no place you can hide," the voice said, "It is just a matter of time." At once I recognized that it was the same voice that had spoken to me at Brookside.

"Who is this?" I demanded. The line went dead.

"Is anything the matter?" Ms. Markham asked sweetly.

"Oh no," I lied. "Probably just a wrong number."

Bruce had retrieved some papers from his desk and was returning to the outer office. As I moved away from the door I caught Lydia Markham staring at me or rather, at my diamond.

"Miss Markham, see to it you bring the Pinckney file," Bruce said as he rejoined me.

"Yes sir," she answered getting up to retrieve the record.

Bruce had taken my arm. We headed back down the hall with Miss Markham following closely behind. We entered the boardroom where a group of men and a few women were seated around a large table. Marco Abruzzi and Mr. Stewart had joined them. Miss Markham took her seat at a separate desk and was readying herself to record the minutes. I noticed Charles standing quietly in a corner. Only one seat remained vacant and it was obviously meant for Bruce. I attempted to move past Bruce and take my place next to Charles when to my surprise Bruce took my arm and led me straight to the executive chair. He held it back in a gesture for me to be seated so I had no choice but to sit down. As I did, I mustered up a smile for the dozen or so pair of eyes staring at me. Bruce took his place standing by my side. I was beginning to feel another attack of butterflies coming on.

"Good Morning," Bruce started, "Before we launch into today's agenda, I should like to make several very special announcements. In the first place, I should like Miss Markham to stay on as my permanent secretary." There were several nods of agreement and clearly Lydia Markham was overjoyed at this news and nodding frantically herself.

"Now then," continued Bruce, "For those of you who don't know her, may I present Ashleigh Grant." He had moved directly behind me and had placed his hands on my shoulders. "Leigh and I are to be married Friday in a private ceremony at Brookside, and I am especially pleased to announce we are expecting a child in February."

The man certainly knew how to drop a bomb. Everyone in the room sat speechless and staring, all but open-mouthed, at us. Even I was shocked by his words but played along in response to the 'warning' I was receiving courtesy of his fingertips on my shoulder blades. I merely smiled and attempted to look like a radiant, prospective bride. He had made no attempt to reveal the details of our relationship. I was sure that many seated in the group had questions, such as how long had we dated or where had we met, but no one had the nerve to ask. It was not unusual, however, that they would not pry into their boss' life, at least not in front of him. I could imagine the flurry of gossip that would soon be filling the halls. Not surprisingly, Marco was the first to regain his composure.

"Congratulations," he said as he came forward to shake Bruce's hand. We now received a barrage of congratulatory remarks and handshakes. Miss Markham looked positively ill and I suspected she was hoping to be appointed to more than just the post of secretary. After several minutes of excitement, the mood again became calm. Bruce shifted gears into business mode and led the meeting with great ease. He, like Nora, knew how to work a crowd. He made his way confidently around the table, stopping near this person and that and calling for their reports. He listened attentively, made comments and opened the floor to lively discussion. I was fascinated by him and was thrilled at the chance to sit in on the meeting. After some time he called a break for an early lunch. He took me aside.

"Darling," he started, "We've a great deal more to cover and I shouldn't want you to have to sit through it. I so wanted you to be here this morning, especially during my announcements." At this he raised an eyebrow and gave me a smile. "I'll join you and Rob for an early supper after which we'll have drinks on the balcony. After all, we've a great many preparations to make for Friday."

"I should say so," I commented, "But by Friday? Don't you think…."

"I promise we'll talk about that later," he interrupted, smiling, "Now enjoy your lunch and tour."

After a peck on the cheek he handed me over to Charles who was to drive me to my lunch date with Nora. On the way out I marveled at the developing relationship between Bruce and myself. I wondered why he wanted to be married so soon. We had known each other for about seventy-two hours and yet he acted as if he had known me for years. I wondered what Nora would make of the fast-paced time schedule.

Charles and I exited the building and he left me waiting at the front door with Peter until he returned with the car. I was informed that a twenty-minute drive would see me lunching with my friend. During the trip my mind kept replaying the earlier scene in the boardroom. Bruce was decidedly a man of great contemplation, sound judgment and common sense or so I had thought. There was obviously a reason for the 'bomb' that had been dropped and for the hurried pace in which the wedding ceremony would take place. I found myself wondering just how I really fit into the equation. Charles stopped the car at a pub, which overlooked the Thames. It was a charming spot for lunch. I could hear Nora's voice before I had even exited the car.

"Leigh, darling," she said as she came running up. She warmly embraced me. "Well, just look at you," she declared, "You look positively radiant. Now this is what I like to see," she said smiling. She had put an arm around me and was guiding me inside. Once indoors she summoned the maitre d.

"Tommy, a private table overlooking the river today," she commanded. The man bowed and beckoned us to follow. After we had been seated and our orders placed, Nora took my hands and touched my ring.

"You have made the right decision," she said, "I know this is a very confusing time, but you will come to see that I am right."

"Do you really think so?" I asked, "Do you realize I'll have known the man for less than one week by the time I walk down the isle? We are to be married on Friday. It's true I feel very comfortable and safe and natural around Bruce and Rob. But is that really reason enough to accept a marriage proposal? So much has happened. Maybe I should…"

"Leigh," she interrupted, "Don't second guess yourself or overanalyze this. Trust me. I know…"

She broke off suddenly. She was no longer looking at me but rather past me at something or someone behind me. As inconspicuously as I could, I shifted in my seat so I could follow her gaze. She seemed to be looking at a man seated a few tables away.

"Is anything wrong?" I inquired.

Regaining her composure she said, somewhat staged, "Oh no, love. That gent is a former client of mine. We just had a difference of opinion, that's all."

Something about her explanation didn't ring quite true, but she gave me no opportunity for further inquiry. She launched into a discussion of Friday's ceremony and all the preparations necessary to make it a success. It was decided that we would start out early the next morning to shop for dresses – mine and hers as she was to be my maid of honor, again. We didn't linger. We paid our check and rose to depart.

It was then that I stole a good glimpse of the man whose presence had slightly unnerved Nora. He was well dressed but wore a scowl on his face. I noted that he had an unmistakable scar running from temple to chin on the left side of his face. I also observed that Charles, who had come to collect us, had taken notice of the man. It was definitely not my imagination. Something was going on, but whatever it was, revelation was not forthcoming from my companions.

Charles ushered us toward the car and Nora began running through the itinerary of the brief walking tour we would take. She had mapped out a route close to Spenceworth's that included much of London's core. Charles let us off at the National Gallery which was to be our starting point. Nora decided that he should stay with the car circling our route and watching for us at our final stop, Ten Downing Street, or pick us up sooner if I became too tired to continue. I had insisted that I could go the distance but she dismissed my protestations by saying that her decision was final. I knew better than to press it further as she had always been a very determined person, especially when her mind was made up.

The National Gallery housed thousands of paintings whose artists spanned many continents and periods of time. There was no way to take in the entire collection in a single viewing but we thoroughly enjoyed the treasures we did see. Practically next door was the National Portrait Gallery with its fascinating collection of a history of England through its people – the famous and the eccentric. We left and went some distance to one of London's most well known symbols, Buckingham Palace home of the royal family. Nora explained that the royal standard was not flying at the masthead as the Queen was typically away during August and September and that the ceremony of the changing of the guard could be seen at precisely the same time daily at certain times of the year. The exterior of the building itself did not strike me as an architectural wonder but I was awestruck by the hundreds of years of history it represented.

We had been standing in the square taking in the building and the people. It was a typically overcast day and it began to rain slightly. Nora retrieved two umbrellas from her bag, passing one to me. We took cover and pressed on skirting the borders of St. James' Park almost doubling back, heading toward the Thames and the Houses of Parliament with their famous clock tower. Nora said that the view of the buildings and their clock tower from the other side of the river might possibly be one of the most famous and photographed views in London and she promised I would see it from that vantage point one day soon.

We did not join the groups waiting on line for a tour of the Houses of Lords and Commons but rather continued just around the corner to Westminster Abbey. The landmark building was truly an amazing sight and I asked Nora if we could peek inside. We went in and ventured forward into the nave. There was no religious ceremony at that time of day but I noted that there were many people present, some saying prayers and some obviously tourists. Nora whispered quietly that the original abbey was built in the eleventh century and had been rebuilt and restored. She explained that most of Britain's monarchs were crowned there and that the building was renowned for royal weddings and funerals with many royals and famous British nationals being buried there. The huge stained glass windows, sculptures and carvings were almost overwhelming to my senses. I imagined that the abbey must be spectacular with the organ playing and a choir singing. I glanced at my watch and saw that well over three hours had passed since we had begun and I was starting to feel a little fatigued.

Nora had taken my arm and was leading me toward an exit saying that we were very close to Ten Downing Street, official residence of Prime Minister Thatcher. As we approached the building I spotted Charles and our car and I admitted, only to myself, that this was indeed a welcome sight. I thanked Nora for her excellent choice of sights and praised her skills as a tour guide.

"A second job perhaps?" She laughed, "Well I'm thrilled that you've enjoyed it. There is so much more to see and I will put together another tour for us to take soon. Now, I must hand you back to Charles and I'll see you tomorrow," she said, hugging me goodbye. She waved as she walked off down the street and Charles and I made our way to the car.

Back at the company offices we spent only a moment with Bruce.

"Darling," he said, "Regrettably we are going to run late. Charles will conduct your tour of the building and then see you home to Brookside. I'll join you as soon as I'm able. I want to hear all about how your afternoon went."

"Very well," I replied. I had been looking forward to watching him in action again, but I was confident that I would enjoy my tour of the offices with Charles. I found myself growing quite fond of him. He was loyal, trustworthy and dependable and always ready to serve the family's needs. In that way he reminded me of my own father.

Bruce had embraced me. Suddenly, we were interrupted by Marco. Neither one of us had heard or seen him approaching.

"Forgive me," he began, "Patrick and Edward have arrived Bruce and we are ready to resume." He made a slight bow in my direction and said, "Enjoy your tour, my dear?"

I smiled acknowledging the question and quickly turned away to join Charles. We made our departure from the executive fifth floor. The fourth floor contained other company offices such as purchasing, accounts payable and receivable, customer service and the like. Floors three and two were showrooms of a sort. Merchandise had been set out and attractively displayed. The inventory was vast and unique – everything from furnishings to jewelry to collectibles.

I enjoyed walking through the displays and watching prospective customers do the same. Charles, in his usual fashion, was an excellent guide. He briefed me on the store's history, its position of prominence in England and Edinburgh, as well as the world, and he pointed out some of the more notable items in the inventory as we went along. We finished up on the first floor, which was partially subterranean. This level was used for receiving and shipping merchandise and also housed the inventory and control office. We had just viewed the warehouse section of the floor when we heard a loud creaking sound. Simultaneously we both realized that within seconds we'd be buried beneath several large crates.

# CHAPTER SEVEN

Before I knew what had happened Charles had pulled me out of harm's way. By doing so, his shoulder was partially clipped by a falling box. The force of the impact threw him off balance and he fell to his knees.

"Oh, Charles!" I cried, moving to his side, "Are you hurt?"

"It's nothing Leigh," he answered, rising slowly and showing me he could move his arm.

We stood silently, staring at the falling boxes. At once people came running and shouting from every direction. Within minutes Bruce was on the scene.

"Leigh!" he cried.

"No, I'm fine, it's Charles who was hit" I said.

"How bad?" Bruce inquired.

Charles merely shook his head. He was unlike any man I had ever met. He was quite composed and despite having been hurt it was obvious he did not want to be fussed over. Bruce and Charles huddled around me like bodyguards, quietly talking amongst themselves. Bruce asked to see the supervisor on duty. A man came forward greeting the men and introducing himself to me as Harry Walker.

"Begging your pardon Madam, Mr. Spenceworth," he began, "Don't know how this happened. Been training a new warehouseman, we have. Believe he mayn't have stacked these crates just so. Put a call out for him and will have words with him soon as he's found."

"Right Harry," said Bruce, "See you have a report for me as soon as possible."

Then to me he said, "Leigh, please say something."

"I'm all right…thanks to Charles," I answered, smiling gratefully at the man.

"Yes, thank heaven for Charles," Bruce replied, gingerly touching Charles' shoulder. Despite all the praise being cast upon him, Charles merely smiled and bowed slightly in our direction.

"Charles, inform Marco he's to conduct the afternoon meetings. I'll ring up later to review. Are you able to bring the car round front? I want Dr. Thompson to have a look at both of you."

"Yes, of course," acknowledged Charles and he set off to carry out his mission.

Bruce guided me to a chair. "Darling, I am going to use the telephone in the office. I'll only be a moment."

I nodded and watched him go. Several employees were still standing around the scene, some talking and others cleaning up the debris.

"Boss thinks its scarface what done it," I overheard one of the men saying.

"Odd sort, he is," another man agreed, "Wouldn't surprise me at all. Worked on the early shift, he did."

At once I thought of the man I had seen during my lunch with Nora. I wondered if he were somehow the perpetrator. But why? Hadn't it just been an unforeseeable accident? Or had someone deliberately arranged the crates haphazardly with the intent of harming Charles and myself? But who had known we'd be touring the building that day? Even if someone had set the crates precariously, it stood to reason he would need a helper on the inside to make them topple over because the crates fell at precisely the moment we passed them and the accused was apparently not on the premises at that moment. I carefully studied the employees that had gathered around looking for a possible suspect. Bruce and Harry had emerged from the tiny office and were making their way toward me.

"Harry, you are to finish your investigation and ring me at Brookside," Bruce was saying.

"Yes sir, Mr. Spenceworth," the man replied.

Bruce escorted me to the front door. News of the accident had apparently traveled fast. Many employees stood staring while others approached us, offering comforting words. Once outside, I drew a deep breath. The fresh air seemed to revive me. We climbed into the car and Charles sped off.

"Dr. Thompson is expecting us," Bruce explained.

"I'm sorry to take you from your meeting," I said.

"Ashleigh, no meeting is more important than you and the baby," he said incredulously. The concern in his voice was so genuine that one would have thought I was his wife and was carrying his baby.

"I know you care. It means everything," I said.

He moved closer and put an arm around me. Eventually we arrived at the Thompson place. The doctor and Mrs. Thompson were waiting at the door. She escorted Charles to one examination room and me to another. After examining us, the doctor pronounced us both in the clear and said that a quiet evening at home with a good hot soak in the tub should restore us both completely. I was relieved to hear that Charles' wound was nothing more than superficial.

"Bruce," I said as we walked toward the car, "I'm feeling much better. Why don't you just drop me off at the house and head back to the office? There's still time to rejoin the meeting."

"Leigh, please do not worry about anything. Marco will handle things. I am going to work from home and then join you and Rob for that early supper. You are to take it easy and Charles is going to take the night off. Perhaps tea in the garden for you and then a leisurely stroll," he suggested.

It sounded like just what the doctor ordered. By the time we arrived at Brookside it was well past teatime. The household was slightly surprised to see us at that hour and even more shocked to hear about what had happened. We parted ways in the foyer with Bruce headed to his study, Charles to his room and me to the garden. Mrs. Major served me as I sat in the rose arbor behind the house. The day had been lovely and now as late afternoon wore on, I sat watching the light starting to fade and listening to the sound of the water dancing in the fountain. Mrs. Major came to clear away.

"Mr. Spenceworth has had to return to the office. He will try to be here for supper," she said.

"Thank you, Mrs. Major," I replied, and then I called after her, "Did Charles go too?"

"He was going to take Mr. Spenceworth into town and then come back," she said.

Bruce had had to make many sudden trips to the

office and at all hours. I wondered what could be so urgent about an import or an export. Like all businessmen I supposed he had deadlines and schedules to meet and he would work whatever amount of time was necessary to achieve them.

I had been sitting at a table, which was underneath a large and ornate metal gazebo covered in climbing roses, only one of the many theme flowers throughout the vast maze-like garden behind the house. The garden consisted of many sections, each seemingly dedicated to a specific flower or color. I stood up and leaving my shady haven, started to follow the stone path that wound its way throughout the floral oasis.

I enjoyed looking at the many types of wild flowers and shrubs. I had never been particularly good with flowers but had always admired a well-manicured garden, so I deeply appreciated the talents and time it took to create and maintain such a thing of beauty. As I walked, I passed underneath several arched trellises covered with vines or roses. Along the path there were several man-made pools with iron benches placed next to them. The garden's beauty rivaled that of a fairy tale. I made a mental note to spend as much time there as I could, delighting in the beauty and serenity it had to offer.

Suddenly I caught a glimpse of someone on the path ahead of me. It was a woman, and at first glance I thought it was Mrs. Major. As I called out, the figure stopped and turned toward me. I came to a full stop, shocked to discover that the woman looking back at me was none other than the woman whose portrait hung above the staircase – Mrs. Spenceworth. I shut my eyes in disbelief. I opened them to find her still standing there, looking at me. She said nothing but motioned for me to follow. I shut my eyes again believing she must be a figment of my exhaustion. Once more I opened them to find her still standing on the path, beckoning me to follow.

Slowly I began to move toward her. At once she began to move as well. I quickened my pace so I would not lose her. I followed her through the garden and out onto the lawn. She was headed toward the family cemetery. Although she did not seem menacing in any way, feelings of fear were taking me over. I watched as she entered the mausoleum. I hesitated at the door. I was very afraid of what I might find inside. However, I summoned courage from somewhere and entered the building. No one was present and nothing seemed disturbed. What could I have seen, I wondered? I began looking at the markers on the stone sarcophaguses. There were several in the room elevated by stone pedestals. Bruce's parents and grandparents lie there. And so did Mrs. Spenceworth. Her interment appeared undisturbed. There was certainly no place to hide in the room, so to where had my quarry disappeared?

As I turned to leave, I took notice of a very large altar at the far end of the room, probably used for commemorative masses. Obeying a hunch, I moved closer to investigate and as I circled around toward the back I saw a door standing ajar. Curious, I opened it the rest of the way expecting to find supplies or linens for church services. Instead, I discovered a subterranean staircase. I hesitated only a moment before bending down to fit through the dwarfed opening. The stone staircase was lit by electric lanterns making me conclude that the passage was frequently used. But, by whom? Bruce? Rob?

When I reached the bottom there was only one way to go. I quietly moved along the underground tunnel. It had been carved out of stone. There were wooden support beams against the walls and in the ceiling every few feet; lanterns hung from these overhead beams. Every now and again I paused and listened. I could hear nothing except my own rapid breathing. All at once I came upon a wooden door, flush with the wall. I turned the knob but the door was locked. Just beyond the door there was a small recess in the stone, which housed a table. Several items were laying on it and I moved closer to examine them. There was a striking portrait of a mother and child, some miniature oil paintings, various tools and a sack. It seemed an odd place for such obviously valuable pieces. Perhaps they were to be locked behind the wooden door. The house was at least three hundred years old according to Bruce. The secret tunnel may have provided a place to secure treasures or a place to hide from persecution in days gone by. I tried the doorknob one more time just to satisfy myself that it was really locked.

I moved on and sometime later realized I had come to the end of the tunnel as I stood facing a wall. It made no sense to me that the tunnel did not somehow connect with another building or even the main house. I combed the wall looking for a secret lever. I found nothing. I did, however, notice what looked like a light switch. I pushed the button expecting to extinguish the lanterns in the passage, but instead a portion of the wall before me suddenly swung backwards toward me. I quickly jumped back out of its way. As I peered through the opening now in front of me I realized that Bruce's study lay on the other side. I stepped through the portal to discover I was entering the room through the fireplace. Its rear wall was actually a secret door! As I stood there looking at the fireplace the door swung shut. It must have been rigged with some type of a time delay. Suddenly, I heard Charles' voice behind me.

"I didn't hear you come in Leigh," he said.

I started and whirled around. "I…I…" was all I could manage.

"Leigh, what is it? Are you feeling poorly?" he asked.

"I need to lie down," I answered, suddenly feeling very weak.

"I'll summon Dr. Thomps…"

"No, no! That really is not necessary," I begged, "I'm…just exhausted." I felt certain from his actions and conversation that he was unaware of my discovery.

He took me by the arm and guided me from the study. We met Mrs. Major in the foyer. She looked from Charles to me, but asked no questions. She merely took my other arm and the three of us climbed the staircase. I made a point of looking at the portrait during our ascent, but it appeared normal. My escorts were extremely hesitant about leaving me at my door, but I insisted.

"Please," I implored them, "There is no need to call Bruce or Dr. Thompson. It has just been an exhausting day and I need a nap before dinner. I promise I'll call if I need help."

They looked at me and then at each other. Somewhat tentatively, they withdrew. Once inside my room I made straight for the bed, not even bothering to undress. My head hit the pillow and I blacked out.

It didn't take me long, when I awoke, to realize that

I'd missed dinner and that it was now the middle of the night. I wondered what commotion, if any, my absence from dinner had caused among my housemates. Perhaps none. After all, who wouldn't be exhausted after the day I'd had, hell, after the week I'd had. I arrived on Monday and it was now the wee hours of Thursday morning. In three days I had become an expectant mother, had received and accepted a marriage proposal, had narrowly escaped serious injury, believed I had encountered a ghost and had discovered a secret tunnel, which I decided would bear watching. I would have to devise a plan for keeping an eye on the visitations to Bruce's study and I most definitely needed to spend more time in the garden to view the comings and goings to the mausoleum. The week was shaping up like the plot from a dime store novel. What would be next?

Almost on cue, I heard a car door. I sat up and lit the lamp next to my bed. The mantel clock read two-thirty. Quickly, but quietly, I slipped from my room. I made my way to the lavatory as one of its windows provided a view of the front courtyard. By the light of the moon, I saw Charles helping Bruce from the car. They headed toward the front door. Where had they been returning from at this hour?

A growing uneasiness took me over. I believed I was a fairly good judge of character and here were two men on whom I'd bestowed my friendship and trust, one of whom I was about to marry. Yet, I'd caught them in the act of being secretive and not just once. Their ambiguity was beginning to unnerve me. I swiftly made my way back to my room, and that was fortunate because I had barely doused the light and climbed into bed when I heard my door opening. I lay very still, pretending to be asleep. Again by the light of the moon, I saw someone advancing toward the bed. It was all I could do to lay still. I scarcely took a breath. As the figure came closer I could see that it was Bruce. Still, I feigned sleep. He sat on the edge of the bed and gently stroked my hair. He began to speak softly.

"Leigh," he whispered, "I will make everything right, I swear. I will avenge both our houses."

I hadn't the least idea what he was talking about and some inner voice warned me to remain silent. He said nothing more and took himself quietly away. I lay there wondering what would become of myself and my unborn child.

# CHAPTER EIGHT

I HAD DRIFTED off to sleep but was being awakened by a gentle prodding. It was Nora.

"Leigh," she was saying softly, "Come on, sleepy head, wake up!"

"Okay, all right," I said looking up at her and mustering a smile, "What time is it?"

"Just after nine o'clock," she answered.

"Nine o'clock!" I echoed, "Why on Earth didn't someone wake me earlier?" I sat upright and pushed back the covers.

"Obviously you needed the rest after the day you had yesterday," she replied, "Now, I'm going downstairs for one of Charles' famous omlettes while you ready yourself for our shopping trip. You still feel up to it, don't you?"

"Oh…yes," I answered absent mindedly, suddenly remembering Bruce's strange visit during the night and realizing that Nora had obviously caught up on the balance of yesterday's events. She certainly had a way of keeping herself fully informed.

"Excellent. Well now, don't rush," she said as she

made her way to the door. "I'm going to savor every bite of my breakfast. Come down when you're ready."

I looked around the room. I climbed out of bed and went to a window. The windows at one end of the room overlooked meadows on one side of the house, while the windows at the other end of the room overlooked the garden and beyond that, the little church and cemetery. I stood gazing out at the little church, scarcely believing that tomorrow I would become mistress of the mansion. I stood there contemplating my decisions of the past several days. I was aware of my desperate need to belong to a family again. Perhaps that desperation coupled with my grief was overshadowing my judgment. On one hand I felt things were progressing too rapidly and yet, on the other I was excited about the prospect of embarking on a new journey, and the plain cold fact of the matter was that I had nothing to go back to. Regardless of my tentativeness, life was barreling along full speed ahead. I had to find some way of fitting in and moving forward with it. I quickly tidied my room, pulled on some clothes, and made up my hair and face. As I made my way downstairs, I paused on the landing to study the portrait.

"Seen her too, haven't you Leigh?"

I whirled around to find Mrs. Major standing a few steps below me. As usual, I hadn't heard her approach.

I didn't know what to say. I looked from her to the portrait.

We were interrupted by Nora who had come to the foot of the staircase.

"There you are! Come along darling," she called up to me, "We've got a hundred things to do!"

I reluctantly moved to join Nora. Mrs. Major gave me a curtsey and a smile, and with a wink of an eye toward the canvass she moved past me and continued on up the stairs. I stood staring after her, determined to find out what she had meant.

"Ashleigh!" Nora said impatiently.

I hurried down the stairs and joined her in the foyer.

"What is it?" she asked, "You look as if you've seen a ghost."

She couldn't have known just how ironic her choice of words was.

"Do you believe in ghosts Nora?" I asked abruptly. She was looking at me as though I'd cracked. "No, really," I continued, "I just want to know what your opinion is."

"Well," she said, "I haven't had any personal experience with one myself, but I certainly have heard enough stories to substantiate……."

And she launched into this story and that as we headed outdoors to meet Charles. I was almost sorry I had asked her opinion as her narrative continued practically all the way into town. The first chance I had, I changed the subject.

"Nora," I confided, "I'm a bit nervous about tomorrow."

"Well naturally, love" she said laughing, "All brides are…"

"No," I cut in, "This is more than pre-wedding day jitters. I find myself questioning my decisions. Everything is happening so fast."

"Yes, I know," she said seriously, "But please don't worry. Everything will be all right."

She had taken my hands and was looking at me with such sincerity, that I made a resolution in that moment to trust my gut and Nora's advice and embrace the new life that lay before me with all my might. There was no use pining for the past; it was gone. A great deal lay before me, not all of which I understood, but I was ready to focus on fitting into my new family.

Nora and I spent several hours shopping like giddy school girls. We had such fun selecting our gowns and several items for my trousseau and we had done our shopping at Harrods. Nora had insisted on a trousseau, although she remained positively tight-lipped on the subject of a wedding trip, claiming complete ignorance on the topic. As we were exiting the store, Edward Stewart was entering.

"Mr. Stewart!" I called, waving.

He started abruptly and then recognizing us, came toward us. He politely greeted me and moved, rather awkwardly I thought, to embrace Nora. They definitely struck me as an odd couple. Nora whispered something in his ear and then kissed his cheek and he made a hasty departure.

"Just making plans for the evening," Nora said smiling and offering an explanation although I didn't need one.

The lunch hour saw us back at Brookside. We ate a light meal in the breakfast room with Rob, who had been excused from classes for two days because of the impending festivities. As we were finishing, Bruce came in. He kissed Rob and sat down at the table.

"Well, ladies?" he inquired smiling, "How went the shopping excursion?"

Nora and I exchanged glances.

"Oh, we managed to find something to wear," Nora said winking at me. We burst into laughter and Bruce and Rob could not help but join in. Just then, Charles came in. Our mood was infectious – he smiled and then reminded Bruce of our appointment with the priest.

"Indeed," remarked Bruce, "Leigh, you and I must steal away now. The others will join us shortly."

We rose and made our departure by way of paned glass French doors that led from the breakfast room out into the rear gardens. It was a beautiful afternoon, the air was crisp and cool. It was early September. Back in the States, the season would be Fall with all of its traditions and glories. It had always been one of my favorite times of the year. Bruce reached for my hand but said nothing. In silence we approached the chapel.

It was an old, stone structure, small and quaint with stained glass windows. A square, stone steeple rose high above the front door. The building sat on the hill that sloped down toward the river. It was surrounded by trees that looked like they could easily have been a hundred years old and that provided the little building with shade. A black, wrought iron fence ran along the perimeter and the neighboring cemetery, which from the looks of it, had been lovingly maintained. I could tell there were many graves from the number of stone markers. These included plain slabs, crosses and some elaborately carved figures of angels. The grass was freshly cut and flowers had been placed on each grave.

I commented about the attention to detail bestowed upon the site and Bruce informed me that once each month Rob and Mrs. Major put fresh flowers on each grave after the gardeners finished their work. He went on to say that Rob had insisted this be done twelve months of the year, regardless of the weather.

Bruce had spoken with great pride about Rob's actions, and rightly so. From what I had observed the boy was indeed a loving and thoughtful child. I looked at the mausoleum and recalled my recent discovery and adventure there. Bruce must have known of the existence of the secret passage having lived there all of his life. I wondered how to approach that subject with him but also realized it was the wrong moment to do so.

He held the wooden door open for me. Inside the sunlight streaming through the stained glass windows cast a warm glow over the room. There were many rows of wooden pews and an altar that closely resembled the one in the mausoleum. I wondered if it too held a secret and decided it would bear a closer examination when the opportunity presented itself. The room itself was simple and it was precisely its simplicity that made it so charming.

"There you be lad and lassie," said a voice, seemingly from out of nowhere.

"Father Walsh!" exclaimed Bruce, moving toward the altar. I had not noticed the man until he spoke. He had been sitting quietly in the first pew. Now he had risen and was moving to greet Bruce. The two men embraced. The priest was a much shorter and older man than Bruce. He reminded me of a leprechaun.

"Father," Bruce was saying, "May I present Ashleigh Grant."

Smiling, I moved forward to greet him. He embraced me, then took my hands and stepped back.

"Aye, she's a beauty," he said surveying me from head to toe.

"Thank you," I said, somewhat embarrassed.

"I think so too," Bruce chimed in.

"Come now, you two," I said, regaining my composure, "No ganging up on the bride."

Both men burst into laughter and I joined in. The kindly old priest took Bruce and me each by the hand and said, "Come." He deposited us in the pew behind which he had been sitting and then resumed his seat. He sat looking at us for a moment.

"There's to be a child," he stated.

I wondered how he knew. I looked at Bruce who was shifting restlessly in his seat.

"I…we…that is to say…." Bruce began, awkwardly.

"Do not worry lad," said the priest gently, "The whys and wherefores are not what matter. I want you both to promise me these things: respect one another, love your children, never go to bed angry, and do all you can to help your neighbor. Have I your solemn promise lad?"

"Yes," answered Bruce.

"Lass?"

"Yes Father," I answered.

He took our hands. "Go with God and much happiness to you. Oh," he said looking at my stomach, "It'll be a lassie you'll be welcoming this time," he grinned, "Now, off with you and fetch your family for the run through." He got up and began slowly making his way toward the altar. Bruce took my hand and led me outdoors.

"How did he know…?" I started.

"They say he has the gift of prophecy," Bruce replied, "Personally, I have always found him to be accurate."

I wondered just what he had meant by that but could hear the sound of voices and laughter and had no chance to ask for clarification. Soon Rob appeared through the trees followed by Charles, Nora and Mrs. Major. Charles was carrying a box, which he handed to Bruce.

"Everyone," Bruce announced, "I need a moment alone with the bride. We'll join you indoors momentarily."

The group moved inside. Bruce turned to me and handed over the box. As I held it, he lifted the lid. Inside lay a diamond tiara. It was exquisite.

"Every Spenceworth bride has worn this on her wedding day and on the day before during the run through," he explained. He lifted the tiara out of its box and placed it on my head.

"There now," he said stepping back to look at me.

All at once I could feel my emotions bubbling over. Tears welled up in my eyes and several ran down my cheeks.

"Leigh," Bruce said moving closer to me.

"Oh, I'm all right," I replied wiping my face, "It's just that I'm, well, I'm happy and sad and nervous and excited. I feel like a walking bundle of nerves."

"Yes, pre-wedding day jitters and all that," Bruce said nodding, "I must admit I've been experiencing a touch of that myself."

"You!" I gasped in disbelief.

"Yes, even me," he answered. "It's been a very long time since there was a woman in my life." He was very close and preparing to embrace me when suddenly Nora's head popped out from behind the door.

"All right you two lovebirds," she started. The stern look she had donned broke into a smile. "Time enough for that after the ceremony. You two are the main attraction and this gig can't start without you, so if you don't mind?" At the conclusion of her reprimand she disappeared back inside.

Bruce and I looked at each other and burst into laughter. Then, arm in arm, we entered the tiny church. The practice went smoothly with everyone trying to memorize their role. The ceremony was to take place at sunrise the following morning. Nora would be my maid of honor while Rob stood up for Bruce. Charles and Mrs. Major were to be witnesses. With the run through concluded our group made its way back to the house. An early supper had been laid out in the dining room. We ate and drank merrily. Toward the conclusion of the meal Mrs. Major approached me.

"Pardon me, ma'am," she said, "If I may take the Spenceworth tiara now? I'm to fit your veil to it."

I glanced at Bruce who nodded his approval. I removed the dazzling headpiece and handed it over.

"I'll have it done right away and bring it to your room," she announced.

As I was thanking her I noticed that Charles had re-entered the room and was whispering something to Bruce, who rose from his chair.

"I'm afraid I need to make a trip to the office," he announced. "I want to thank you all for taking part in this special day." He began to make his way around the table. He hugged Rob and Nora.

"Until sunrise," he said to me softly. Bruce had agreed to a sunrise ceremony as it had always been my favorite time of day. It was not only the beauty and tranquility of the early morning that was special to me, but also that it brought the chance for a new beginning. It somehow seemed very fitting to our circumstances. Bruce took his leave followed closely by Charles.

I couldn't help but wonder what pressing business matter again demanded his attention. Following a sudden impulse I ran after them and stopped them in the foyer.

"Bruce, what is it?" I inquired as calmly as I could.

The two men glanced at each other, and then Bruce said, "Please don't worry. Harry rang up about the business in the warehouse."

"Can't it keep until morning?" I asked.

"I'm afraid it cannot," he replied. "And nothing will interfere with our plans for tomorrow." He looked intently at me and then his gaze shifted over my shoulder.

It was then that I realized that Nora had followed us into the foyer and had overheard the conversation. Now I caught an unreadable glance thrown by Bruce in her direction. She came forward and put an arm around me.

"Come love," she coaxed, "Let's you and I retire for the evening." She was steering me toward the staircase. I glanced back over my shoulder to see Bruce and Charles depart.

"Nora…." I said, as we started our ascent but she cut me to the quick as if reading my mind.

"My dear, you have had a long and busy day. And tomorrow is your wedding day. Now, no more serious conversation. I'm taking you upstairs, drawing your bath and seeing you to bed!" she announced.

Although I wanted the answers to several questions, I allowed myself to be silenced. Nora was as good as her word. She fussed over me, chatted endlessly about this and that, and then tucked me into bed. I must have fallen asleep quickly, but was awakened some time later perhaps by nerves or preoccupation with my situation or by some sound. Whatever it was I decided I could not get back to sleep without a warm glass of milk. I crept quietly from my room, down the hall and down the staircase. As I neared the bottom I noticed Bruce's study light was switched on and the door was standing slightly ajar. I could hear voices – Charles and Bruce. I decided to enter and talk with them. As I approached the door I overheard Charles say, "When will you tell Leigh?" I stopped in my tracks. I listened for Bruce's response. "The time is not right," he said, "But soon, very soon."

As I stood there contemplating what to do next, I heard a familiar swooshing sound. I burst through the door just in time to see the fireplace's secret door swing shut. So, they were the ones using the secret passage! I hadn't had enough time the day I discovered the passage to examine the mantel for the secret lever that allowed access from the study. Now, try as I would, I could not find it. Dejected, I turned to leave but then heard a sound behind me. As I looked back I expected to see the door swinging open. Instead, I saw Mrs. Spenceworth standing before me. This time I tried hard not to blink, but rather to watch her every move. She took a step toward the fireplace and stretched out a hand, touching the head of one of the cherubs carved in stone. The rear wall of the fireplace swung open.

I stood, I'm sure, open-mouthed as the scene unfolded before my eyes. I blinked hard and upon opening my eyes discovered I was alone in the room. As I hastened through the opening I decided that Mrs. Spenceworth was a friendly sort of spirit. I could not explain why, but I felt certain she was an ally. After all, her actions had thus far been helpful and informative. I hurried along the tunnel. I could still hear muffled voices ahead. Then, the sound of a door opening. I came upon the wooden door that had been locked during my previous visit. It was standing open. Behind it stood a metal door with no knob or apparent way to gain entry. Suddenly I noticed a small keypad mounted on the door jam. The realization that I was no longer standing in any ordinary dusty old passage was dawning on me rather sharply. I became afraid to be there and quickly retraced my steps, re-entering the study. I made my way to my room and locked the door.

What was going on? What could Charles and Bruce be up to? Midnight outings, secret passages......Suddenly I noticed my wedding veil laying on the dresser. Mrs. Major had delivered it according to her word. She had indeed managed to attach my long, multi-layered veil to the delicate diamond tiara. I placed it on my head and moved in front of the mirror. The headdress was so remarkably beautiful that I smiled in spite of the overwhelming sense of apprehension I was feeling. I said to my reflection, "What am I doing?" It was then that I saw her standing behind me. I whirled around to find myself face to face with Mrs. Spenceworth for the second time that evening.

I didn't bother to close and reopen my eyes as I'd grown convinced by earlier encounters that she was actually there. Previously, however, I had not been so close to her. She seemed so real that I could not help but stare, and she in turn was staring at me. I remembered that I was wearing the tiara and I began to fear she might be angry about my use of it or the impending nuptials. I quietly removed the headpiece and my action caused her to smile.

"I'm confused," I said aloud, voicing my inner thoughts, "You must have come for a reason." I paused wondering if communication was possible. "Can you speak?"

"Trust in Bruce," came the answer.

I was so startled by the fact that she had actually spoken that I stepped backwards and in so doing, bumped into a chair. I reached back for it and sank down into it, never once taking my eyes from hers. I was truly speechless. She smiled again and then vanished, right before my eyes.

"Don't leave!" I pleaded, finding my voice. From somewhere in the darkness the words came again, "Trust in Bruce." I sat there for some time watching, listening, thinking. An unexplainable calm settled over me. Eventually I climbed into bed and fell asleep.

# CHAPTER NINE

We were married at sunrise. Nora and Elizabeth Major had awakened me very early. They helped me dress and make my way to the ancestral chapel on the hill. Bruce, Charles and Rob were there waiting at the altar with Father Walsh. Dr. and Mrs. Thompson were also present. There was no music as Nora and I processed down the aisle, but our path had been covered with the petals from what must have been dozens of yellow roses. I knew instantly it had been a loving gesture made by Rob. He was smiling from ear to ear as I looked at him to acknowledge his thoughtfulness with my own smile and a wink. As the sun slowly rose, Bruce and I recited our vows, exchanged rings and were pronounced man and wife. We were showered with congratulatory cheers from family and friends. Arm in arm Bruce and I left the chapel surrounded by our small group.

We made our way back to the house. A breakfast wedding feast had been laid out in the formal dining room. Bruce had hired a caterer so that Charles and Mrs. Major could partake in the celebration, although several times I caught each one of them watching the caterer's work with a critical eye. Bruce escorted me to my chair and then took his own opposite mine. He raised his glass, "To Mrs. Spenceworth!" Our companions had also raised their glasses, "Mrs. Spenceworth!" they echoed. I could scarcely believe the state of happiness that had overtaken me.

The day was filled with excitement as we moved outside for a game of cricket on the lawn. After a highly competitive game of boys against girls, with the girls triumphant, our group strolled leisurely through the gardens and then sat by the river as Bruce read to us from the family journals. Lunch came and went and tea was served early in the rose garden behind the house. Although I was enjoying the day I kept a watchful eye over the gardens, half expecting the first Mrs. Spenceworth to make an appearance. Later in the afternoon, we again gathered in the formal dining room for a light supper.

As the meal drew to a close, Bruce came to me and said, "You'd better change darling. We've quite a trip ahead of us."

"Trip?" I repeated blankly, "Where are we…"

"Our honeymoon," he answered, looking me in the eye.

I could feel the blush spread across my face. Nora burst out laughing.

"Come on, love," she smiled, "I'll help you."

Nora, Mrs. Major and Mrs. Thompson accompanied me to my room where they helped me change and pack a bag. Now I understood why Nora had been so insistent on purchasing items for a trousseau. Suddenly, we heard the sound of a helicopter.

"My goodness," said Mrs. Thompson, "Sounds as if it'll land on the roof."

We stood listening, trying to decipher which direction the machine was headed. The door flung open to admit Rob followed by Bruce. Rob ran straight to me and took my hands, pulling me toward a window.

"Leigh, the helicopter is here!" he exclaimed.

"Is that what's making all the noise?" I asked smiling.

We peered out the window and watched the machine landing on the lawn.

"Your chariot awaits," said Bruce, with a slight bow, "Nora, have you told her or shall I?"

"Told me what?" I demanded looking from one to the other.

"Edward and I are going to join you and Bruce on the second leg of your trip," she said, "I realize that you'll be on your honeymoon but I hope that's all right, love. Now I can't give away any more details but we will see you late tomorrow," she finished, looking from me to Bruce.

"Really? Oh, that would be wonderful!" I cried, moving to embrace her tightly. I said nothing more but she had known me long enough to know that I would be forever grateful. This would be a most unusual honeymoon trip and quite frankly, the more people on it, the better. I felt sure Bruce would see it that way too.

I received warm embraces from Mrs. Thompson and from Rob. Then, hand in hand with Bruce, made my way from the house to the helicopter. The group followed us out onto the lawn and stood waving as we climbed aboard. Although Nora was smiling at us she seemed somewhat anxious. I reasoned that it was one friend's concern for another – we had all been through a most exciting day.

"May I know where we are going?" I asked Bruce as we took our seats.

"We shall spend the night at the family's summer place on the sea, north of here, in Scotland to be precise. And late tomorrow afternoon, Nora and Edward will join us on the train to Edinburgh. Edward and I will conduct some business at our offices there while you and Nora tour the city," was my answer.

"Scotland!" I exclaimed, "Oh Bruce, how wonderful. And how thoughtful of you to invite Nora and Edward."

He smiled and said nothing, but I felt certain he understood my meaning.

Just then Charles climbed aboard, seating himself next to the pilot. Among the many roles Charles Henderson filled, it struck me at that moment that he also filled the role of protector and naturally we should not venture off without his joining us.

Bruce had been helping me to secure my safety belt and headset. As he worked he said, "It should be under two hours flying time Leigh, so do try to sit back and relax."

He strapped himself in, adjusting his own headset and then retrieved his briefcase. He placed it on his lap, opened it and began studying various documents. I settled back and enjoyed taking in the view. I had never flown in such a craft and I appreciated the unique chance to observe the world from such a vantage point. Daylight was fast giving way to dusk and surely by the time we reached our destination it would be dark. At some point during the journey, I drifted off to sleep. All at once I was being gently awakened.

"Leigh, we've arrived," Bruce was saying.

I opened my eyes just in time to see our descent onto another lawn, one that had been lit up by very bright floodlights. Charles and Bruce helped me from the craft and as they did I came face to face with a very large stone castle.

"This wouldn't, by any chance, be that 'summer place' you spoke of?" I asked dryly.

"It is the very same," said Bruce laughing, "Welcome to Mereness Castle of Berwick-Upon-Tweed," he announced formally.

We had been dropped off some distance from the castle. A charming carriage, drawn by a single horse and decorated with white ribbons, stood ready to take us the rest of the way. The massive building stood only feet above sea level. From what I could see, it appeared to rise up from the rocks that supported it. There was beach between castle and ocean, but at high tide the waves must surely hit the building. I must have been studying my new surroundings somewhat awestruck, for suddenly I noticed Bruce and Charles staring at me with wide grins on their faces.

"Well, all right," I said in my defense, "It's not everyday a girl gets married to a man she's known less than a week and then flies by helicopter to a magical castle by the sea!"

The men burst into laughter, despite the validity of my statement, and I joined them. As they heaved the baggage into the carriage I took note of a crude homemade banner reading 'Just Married' that had been fastened to the back of the carriage. Charles took the reigns and then with Bruce and I sitting behind him, started slowly toward the castle. As we got closer,

I could see that we would be crossing a small bridge that stood over a moat, which encircled the building. Bruce explained that presently the moat provided a means of over spill for the sea, so that the castle would not become flooded. In days gone by it had provided additional protection from enemies.

"I cannot believe I am actually going to stay here," I said.

"You were quite right before," Bruce replied, "The place does have a magical quality about it. Built in the 1600s by William Mereness, it has always been maintained by family members. The Spenceworths have had it nearly one hundred years, mostly because we had the foresight to establish a trust for the upkeep. Magical, but damned costly to maintain."

The carriage had crossed the bridge and entered the inner courtyard where we disembarked. Bruce led me toward a door. Suddenly it swung open and we were greeted by an elderly woman.

"Mrs. Arnold!" Bruce exclaimed. He gave the woman a warm embrace. "I didn't expect you to stay."

"Mr. Bruce," she answered, "I'd be no other place, what with you bringing your bride and all. Aye, she's a beauty," she said looking me over.

"Thank you," I said smiling.

"Mrs. Arnold, may I present Ashleigh Spenceworth," Bruce announced ceremoniously. The woman moved to embrace me.

"Welcome lass. Now, you must be positively done in. Your rooms are ready and I've prepared a light snack as ye'll be wanting to retire." As she talked she led the way inside and up a stone staircase. I was indeed very tired and although I very much wanted to absorb every detail of the place, I took only the slightest notice of the interior. As I followed her I wondered just what arrangements had been made for the evening. After all, it was our wedding night.

"There now," Mrs. Arnold was saying as she threw open a door, "The bridal suite with adjoining dressing room. Of course the Mrs. will take the master bed in keeping with tradition and Mr. Bruce, I've made up the bed in the next room." It was as if she had read my mind. And, apparently, so had Bruce as he must have previously instructed her about how to prepare things. The arrangements were indeed unusual for newlyweds, but if the woman thought so, she never let on. On the contrary, she acted as if all were in order.

"Well now," she said, "The fire's lit and your snack is laid out on that table. I've told Mr. Arnold that I'd be staying the night and so ye'll find me downstairs in me room if you should be needing anything."

With a smile and a satisfied nod of her head she left us. The occasional crackle of the fire prevented a totally awkward silence, but there was a tension I was not sure how to handle. I was relieved when Bruce spoke.

"My dear, it is very late. Suppose you prepare for bed first - the loo is just through the dressing room. Meanwhile, I'll busy myself with unpacking and sampling our snack."

He didn't have to ask me twice. I picked up my bag and went through to the bathroom. As I did, I noticed the small bed made up for him. I wondered just what his thoughts were about our situation. There was obviously an attraction between us, but with meeting and marrying so quickly it would take time for all things to fall into place. Yes, time, it seemed to me, was what was needed.

I quickly washed my face and combed my hair and donned a rather striking peignoir that Nora had given me. Taking a deep breath I emerged and made my way back into the bedroom. Bruce was standing near the fire, but upon hearing me enter he turned to look at me. He said nothing but crossed the room, coming to stand very close to me. His closeness made my heart pound faster. He took my hand and pressed it to his lips. I could feel the blush engulf my face. He pulled me to him and kissed me gently on the cheek. He released me and walked toward the dressing room door.

"I'll just be next door if you should need anything," he said quietly, "Goodnight."

"Goodnight Bruce," I answered, watching him disappear through the door. He closed it behind him. I crossed the room and sat in a chair near the fire. On a table next to me was the snack Mrs. Arnold had left. I helped myself to warm milk and a buttered biscuit. I was really not surprised by Bruce's actions. There was a great deal about the man I did not know, but I was fairly certain that he was a gentleman. His sensitive handling of our first night as man and wife only served to deepen my regard for him. Smiling, I climbed into bed and lay there happily recalling the day's events.

# CHAPTER TEN

I MUST HAVE been exhausted because I slept through the night not even bothering to wake, as was my custom on the first night in a strange place. I awoke to find Bruce sitting quietly in a chair next to the bed. I sat up and said, "Good Morning."

"Good Morning to you, Mrs. Spenceworth," he answered smiling, "I thought I'd have Mrs. Arnold serve you a light breakfast in bed, after which I'll take you on a tour of the castle. I thought we would lunch in town as it's only a stone's throw away. It will be a pleasant distraction while we wait for Nora and Edward. Sound good?"

"Sounds wonderful," I replied.

He rose from the chair and walked toward the fireplace. I hadn't noticed it last night, but hanging near to it was a bell rope. He pulled on it once. I listened but heard nothing. Apparently it could only be heard by the one it summoned. Moments later Mrs. Arnold appeared carrying a tray in one hand and a newspaper in the other.

"And a very good mornin' to you, Mr. and Mrs.,"

she said smiling, but gazing rather intently from one to the other of us. I smiled, as did Bruce. She laid the tray and paper down next to me and took herself off without any further conversation.

"Well now," started Bruce, "You enjoy a leisurely breakfast and dress when you're ready. I've several things to see to downstairs. I'll come back for you, in say, three quarters of an hour?"

"That will be fine," I answered. When he had gone, I poured a cup of tea and bit into a scone. I opened the newspaper, one of London's daily's, to find that the 'Creeper' had made headlines yet again. It seemed that the theft had gone undiscovered for some time as the homeowners had been on holiday. The article went on to list the stolen items as mostly artworks. Accompanying the article were photographs of some of the stolen items. A picture of a painting caught my eye. I gazed intently at it feeling certain I had seen it somewhere before. It was the striking painting of mother and child I had seen lying on the table in the secret tunnel at Brookside.

I sat in disbelief, trying hard not to accept what this must mean. Someone at Brookside was the 'Creeper' or was in league with the thief. But who? I was so sure I was truly coming to know the members of the household, the members of my new family. Surely there must be a mistake. I studied the photograph but I was certain in my mind that the painting was the one I had seen in the secret passage.

I sat there trying to decide what to do. Maybe I could reach Nora. I glanced around the room looking for a telephone but did not see one. What would I tell her, 'Oh, by the way I believe I married London's

Creeper?' She would surely think I'd gone over the edge. Fortunately I would be seeing her in a matter of hours. Clearly something was going on at Brookside, but what and who was involved remained to be discovered. I quickly rose and dressed. I was just finishing tidying the room when Bruce returned.

"How are you feeling this morning?" he asked.

His innocent question unnerved me, although there was no way he could have known what had just been on my mind. I realized I'd have to feign the role of the happy bride until I figured out what was going on and who the players were.

"I'm feeling remarkably well," I returned, summoning a smile, "I slept soundly and am looking forward to our tour and to seeing Nora. I trust your accommodations were satisfactory as well?"

He stood looking at me as though trying to process what I had said. I sensed that he was picking up on the edge to my voice and I would have to try harder to act as though nothing was wrong.

He merely said, "Yes, thank you. Shall we get started?" He held the door open for me. I passed through and once in the hallway he took the lead. He was quite an excellent guide, talking about the history of the place and pointing out objects of interest. As the morning wore on I realized, somewhat unhappily, that I was beginning to distance myself from him. Until I had seen the paper I had delighted in being close to him and had looked forward to watching our relationship grow. Now I felt as though we were taking a turn in the wrong direction as my reservations were increasing, given what I had seen in the newspaper. I hoped I was adequately covering up any external signs of my increased anxiety.

We finished the inspection of the castle and made our way, via horse and carriage, to town. Although the castle set atop the rocks next to the sea gave an air of being isolated, the town was only about four miles away. It was quaint with cobbled stone roads and walls, a butcher shop and candy store, and row houses with fenced in gardens. The church and schoolhouse stood side by side. Along the way people waved or shouted a friendly greeting. We stopped the carriage outside Roy's Pub. As we entered a man behind the bar called out, "Welcome Bruce. Up for the weekend, are ye?"

Bruce smiled and said, "It's a very special weekend Roy. I've brought my bride with me."

"Well, I'll be," the man replied as he came out from behind the bar to shake hands with Bruce. "She's a fine lookin' lass. You've done well for yerself boy."

"Thank you Roy," laughed Bruce, "May I present Ashleigh Spenceworth."

"A hundred thousand welcomes to you lass," he said shaking my hand earnestly.

"Thank you very much," I said smiling. I was touched by the sincerity of his greeting. Several people in the establishment had turned to watch the introductions and now had risen and were offering welcomes and congratulatory comments. Soon, we were seated at a large table with a lively group of townspeople that had known Bruce and his family for years. Where I had previously cherished time alone with Bruce, I now was glad, even relieved, that we were not lunching alone. Our impromptu party lasted long beyond the lunch hour with more and more people joining in as they stopped into the Pub. I was having such a good time I had all but forgotten my new-found fears. Suddenly I realized how weary I'd become.

"Bruce," I said quietly, "I am feeling a bit tired. Would you mind terribly if I went back? You are welcome to stay as long as you like."

"It's time we both went back. Nora and Edward should be here," he said, glancing at his wristwatch. He found Roy, shook the man's hand and thanked him profusely for the special afternoon. We rode back to the castle in silence. Up to this point, we had seen nothing of Charles. Now, as we approached the castle I could see that he was waiting for us in the inner courtyard. As we disembarked, he approached Bruce and they had a quick word.

"Leigh," Bruce said, "Nora and Edward have indeed arrived. Why don't you go through? Charles and I shan't be long."

"Yes, of course," I said, smiling at both men as I moved past them. I couldn't get inside fast enough. I came upon Mrs. Arnold first, her arms full of clean linens.

As if reading my mind she said, "Afternoon dear. You're friends are in the parlor."

I thanked her and went in. I had expected to see them both but Nora was sitting alone in an oversized armchair, sipping coffee. I seized the opportunity to talk with her.

"Nora, you'll never believe…" I started but caught myself as Edward came in.

He looked from one of us to the other as if realizing that he had interrupted something.

"I'll never believe what?" Nora asked, setting her mug down on the table next to her chair.

At that moment our threesome grew as Bruce and Charles entered the room.

"You'll never believe how exciting it was spending

the night in a castle," I answered saying the first thing that I could think of.

She looked at me without responding as though my statement struck her as odd.

"Well, now," Bruce said, "Charles informs me we are ready to set off. Shall we then?"

"Oh, rather," Edward answered enthusiastically. He moved closer to Nora and helped her from her chair. She smiled at him as she took his hand and stood up and as I observed their interaction, I couldn't stifle the feeling that there was something odd about their union. I just couldn't figure out what that was.

Mrs. Arnold and a man I assumed to be Mr. Arnold were in the courtyard loading our baggage into a car. My guess that the man was Mr. Arnold had been correct. Bruce informed me that he would be taking us to the rail station. A few minutes later saw the baggage secure, us in our seats and we were off. I was very excited at the thoughts of a scenic rail journey but my elation was overshadowed by my anxiety that someone at Brookside was London's 'Creeper.'

I gazed thoughtfully from Bruce to Charles. Although I had known neither man for long, I simply could not bring myself to believe that either of them could be caught up in something so underhanded. Suddenly I noticed that Nora was watching me. I quickly smiled at her, wondering what she was thinking. Whatever else was going on, I was very glad of her presence, and I could hardly wait to tell her of my concerns and hear what she had to say on the subject.

# CHAPTER ELEVEN

AT THE RAIL station, Mr. Arnold and Charles unloaded the baggage while Bruce and Edward spoke with a porter. Bruce came and took my arm and guided me toward an entry door.

"Have you ever journeyed by rail?" he inquired, as we approached the train.

"Well, only the occasional day trip," I answered, "But never overnight and never on anything luxurious."

"I believe you will enjoy this," he responded, taking my hand and helping me climb the narrow metal stairs. "The train follows the coast through Dunbar and North Berwick and then arrives in Edinburgh. The scenery is spectacular and we sleep over one night. Here, this way." He guided me through what he called Observation Car A. Its interior was filled with plush sofas and armchairs with plaid being the predominant curtain and upholstery theme. There were coffee tables and end tables and reading lamps and standing lamps. The room was as cozy as the sitting rooms at Brookside. Large windows framed by small curtains provided the portals through which we would see the Scottish highlands and the North Sea.

We passed through the coach, followed closely by Edward and Nora and Charles and on through another observation car, so-called Observation Car B, and then on through to the dining car. This car was longer than the others and paneled in rich woods and was filled with tables of all sizes – big enough to accommodate a large group and small enough for only two. The tables were clothed and set with fine china and crystal. I found myself thinking that the ride must be a very smooth and even one to accommodate all that glassware. Every table had candles and a vase containing a bouquet of fresh thistle and greens. The windows in the coach were not as large as those in the observation cars. There were oil paintings of all sizes and shapes attached to the paneling. Beyond the dining car were the sleeping coaches.

Bruce paused to speak with a porter who directed us toward a cabin. Nora and Edward were to be next door to us, and Charles further down the passageway. While Bruce worked the lock on our door, the others passed us and headed down the passageway. A few other travelers moved past us in the narrow hall. A man bumped into me sending me straight into Bruce, who reached out to help steady me. The man mumbled a quick apology but kept moving. I glanced after him but he was wearing a hat, coat and scarf which made it impossible, I thought, for me to recognize him if our paths happened to cross again on the journey.

At last the door was open and Bruce allowed me to enter first. The cabin was small but elegant. Also paneled in rich woods it had brass wall lamps, fine furnishings and plaid upholstery. There was a small double bed, a desk and wash-basin, a ceiling fan, a service call button, a small wall safe and a private bath. I stood looking at the bed, remembering how the night before we each had our own accommodations. Bruce excused himself saying he would return momentarily. I moved toward the window. Passengers of all sizes, shapes and ages were boarding. I wondered just what the train's passenger capacity could be. I wondered what it would be like sleeping in the same bed as Bruce. At that moment, he returned.

"I've just spoken with Nora and Edward. They would be glad to exchange cabins with us," he said quietly.

"Exchange cabins?" I echoed.

"Theirs contains two small twin beds, one at each end of the cabin," he explained. "I thought that under the circumstances, it might be more comfortable," he finished.

"I…that….that would be fine," I managed to say. I could feel the blush spread across my face. I felt very awkward and I wondered how he could remain so calm and seemingly unaffected by the situation. Although it was our honeymoon, we were hardly the typical newlyweds. I was completely embarrassed that he so quickly detected my uneasiness about the bed and I followed him out into the passageway. Nora and Edward were already on their way, baggage in hand. I could scarcely look at them, although I felt certain Nora would understand.

"Edward and I are going to change for dinner," she said cheerfully. "Why don't we meet in Observation Car B and have a drink before dinner in say half an hour?" she suggested.

"I think we'd like that," Bruce answered, "Wouldn't we, Leigh?"

"Yes," I said, "That would be lovely." I was grateful

that they didn't pause any longer but moved across the threshold of their new lodgings.

Bruce opened the door to our new cabin and once again allowed me to pass through first. As I stepped in, I saw that the room was identical to the one we had just left except for the twin beds. It suddenly struck me that this was meant to be Nora and Edward's cabin – a cabin with twin beds. I had thought something seemed odd about the two of them and the room's set up only served to fuel that speculation. If they were an item, a couple in love, what were they doing in separate beds?

"Is everything all right Leigh?" Bruce asked, gazing at me intently.

"Oh yes," I answered quickly. "I wonder how Charles is getting on."

"Quite well, I imagine," he said.

"Yes, I imagine you're right," I agreed. "He seems a remarkable man. Bruce, about Charles, has he a family? I mean a wife or children?"

Bruce paused a moment before responding. "Once upon a time he was married and very much in love. His wife and child died during childbirth. It's a bond we share, but not one that we often speak of."

I didn't know what to say. They had both lost loved ones during childbirth and I could see how the sharing of this could bring them closer together.

"How many passengers can the train carry?" I inquired, changing the subject.

"It's around fifty I believe," he answered. "This one was designed for a small, intimate group."

"Would you like to change first or shall I?" I asked, motioning toward the bath.

We had been at opposite ends of the cabin unpacking our bags. He crossed the small space and came to stand quite close to me.

"Leigh, I'm aware that our situation is a bit unusual at this moment, and I believe that things will change between us," he started, "And I want you to feel secure in the knowledge that I would never force myself, or my attentions, where they weren't welcome," he finished.

"Oh Bruce," I said, taking my hand and resting it on his cheek, "I know that; I can sense that. I'm sorry if I made it seem that I was afraid….I'm just… well, I'm just a bit nervous." I paused before continuing. "I, too, am hoping that in time things will change between us." I heard the words coming out of my mouth but could not believe I had found the courage to say them.

He stepped closer to me, taking my hand from his cheek and bringing it to his lips. His kiss sent shivers up and down my spine. He put his other arm around me, pulling me closer. Just then there was a knock at the door and he moved to answer it.

It was Charles. "Mr. Spenceworth, may I have a word?" He asked. Bruce nodded. "I trust Mrs. Spenceworth is doing well." Bruce took a step backward while opening the door further. He gestured toward me with the other hand.

"Oh yes, Charles, thank you," I answered, smiling at him. "And you? All settled in?"

"Yes, Madame," he said.

"Leigh," Bruce said, moving through the door, "I shan't be long. You change first then and would you lay out my evening suit?"

"Yes, I will," I said, moving toward the door and watching them go down the passageway. At that moment there was a sudden jolt as the train began to move, slowly at first and gradually climbing in speed.

I stepped backward into the cabin, shut the door and moved toward his bed. I unzipped his carry bag and removed the evening suit. It seemed like such a domestic thing to do – to ready the husband's clothes. I stood there reflecting on how much I liked his touch and how it made my heart race to look into those green eyes. The telephone rang.

Somewhat apprehensively, I picked up the receiver. "Hello?"

"Leigh, darling," started Nora, "Edward and I will be leaving our room soon. How are you and Bruce coming along?"

"We're fine," I answered, relieved to hear Nora's voice, "Bruce has gone to see Charles but should be back soon. Listen, Nora, we need to talk. After dinner let's find a way to slip away from the men for a while."

"Okay, darling, I'm anxious to hear all about how the honeymoon is going," she laughed. "We'll see you soon."

"Yes, we'll be along shortly," I promised, putting back the receiver. She had misunderstood what I wanted to talk about but then how could she know? I was almost bursting at the seams to tell her about the secret passage at Brookside, what I'd seen in it and the possible connection to the article in the paper.

I picked up my evening gown and went into the bath to change. The gown was a three-quarter length dress of an ivory color. It was a sleeveless silk dress with a chiffon long sleeve top layer that had been decorated with opalescent sequins. Nora had spied it during our pre-wedding shopping trip and had insisted that it would come in handy for some occasion. I wasn't long and when I opened the door, I saw Bruce sitting on his bed. He looked extremely preoccupied, almost anxious. He stood up, smiling, when he realized I was watching him.

"You look beautiful," he said.

"Thank you," I replied, feeling slightly self-conscious.

"I'll be a moment," he promised, gathering up his evening wear and heading for the bath, closing the door behind him.

I walked back and forth in the small area wondering what he and Charles could have talked about that had him looking so worried. He reappeared a short time later, immaculately dressed in a white dinner jacket with a white shirt and black trousers. His necktie and pocket handkerchief were plaid. He seemed to have regained his composure, apparently having stifled whatever was troubling him.

"You look very handsome," I said.

He took my hand and led me toward the wall mirror. We stood in front of it, looking at our reflection. He was behind me and he put his arms around my waist.

"Quite a nice looking couple," he boasted, "Wouldn't you agree?"

"Yes," I agreed. As I stood there looking at the two of us I realized that I didn't want to believe Bruce could be involved in the London 'Creeper' business, not my Bruce. I suddenly thought of the previous Mrs. Spenceworth and half expected her to appear in the reflection as well. I was relieved that she didn't but wondered why thoughts of her were so strong.

"Everything all right with Charles?" I inquired as innocently as I could.

"Oh yes," he replied. He said it casually enough but also with a tone of finality that seemed to warn me not to press the issue at that moment. He let me go and crossed the tiny space to open the door.

"Shall we?" he inquired, gesturing toward the open doorway. I nodded, crossed the cabin and exited first.

After closing and locking the door, he led the way toward Observation Car B. The crossing between cars was slightly rough with the train moving but Bruce held on to me tightly. Once inside the coach, we quickly located Nora and Edward and made our way toward them. They were seated in a cozy corner where two sofas faced each other. There was an end table next to each one with a lamp on it. Edward was seated on one couch and Nora on the other. He stood up acknowledging me with a nod of the head and shaking hands with Bruce.

"Well, old man, you're looking quite elegant," he said, patting Bruce on the shoulder. "And Mrs. Spenceworth, may I say that you look radiant."

"Oh, thank you," I responded, "And please, call me Leigh."

"Oh yes," he said.

"Nora, you are looking gorgeous, as usual," Bruce said to her. She smiled and laughed at the compliment.

"Thank you, darling," she answered. "Well, do sit down and Edward, summon the waiter, will you love? Let's get Leigh and Bruce fixed up with a drink"

While Edward carried out Nora's bidding, I took a seat next to her. After he and Bruce had placed our drink order, the men took their seats on the couch facing us. It was dusk but there was still enough daylight to see the passing landscape.

"Oh," I exclaimed, pointing toward the window. "Look at that!" Outside, across the water on a small island, stood a castle.

"Oh yes," said Bruce, "We will pass several more before reaching Edinburgh." He went on to explain that most of them were still lived in and in good repair. I thought it must have been very exciting to live year round in those stone structures for they contained hundreds of years of history, not to mention having such breathtaking views to look at every day. I started to think about how different the landscape here was in comparison to where I had come from, but quickly cut myself off from that line of thought.

Our foursome engaged in some lighthearted conversation and watched the Scottish highlands pass by twilight. About forty minutes later saw us seated in the dining car, which was fast filling up. Nora and I had chosen a salmon and rice dish, while the men had selected a beef and potato entrée. Nora had insisted that we share a bottle of champagne with the meal in celebration of the honeymoon. I inquired after Charles and was informed by Bruce that he would take supper in his cabin. The cuisine was exquisite and the conversation had no problem moving along but several times I had the feeling that each one of my dinner companions was expecting to see someone they knew. No one was looking around the coach in an obvious way; it was subtle, but they were definitely looking for something. When the meal concluded, Bruce and Edward excused themselves. I seized my opportunity.

"Nora," I said, "Did you know there is a secret passageway at Brookside?"

For a moment she almost looked startled but she quickly regained her composure.

"Really?" she answered, "Well, I suppose a house that old could have a few. How do you know?" Her question might have seemed like a casual inquiry to one who didn't know her better, but I'd known her a long time.

"You do know about it!" I exclaimed. She admitted nothing and I plowed on, not revealing how I'd discovered the secret tunnel. "I stumbled across a passage that connects the family mausoleum to the house and there were some paintings laying on a table and a picture of one of them was in the newspaper. It was stolen by the 'Creeper' and that must mean that someone at Brookside is the… is the…" I faultered as I noticed Bruce and Edward approaching the table. It must have been obvious by our expressions that they were interrupting something.

"Everything all right?" Bruce inquired, looking from one to the other of us.

"Oh yes," Nora answered, laughing, "Leigh and I were just discussing all of the juicy honeymoon details."

I was positively embarrassed by her statement and annoyed that our conversation had been cut short.

"Right," said Edward. "Well, if you'll excuse us, Nora and I are going to make an early evening of it."

Nora looked as if his statement was news to her but she rebounded quickly, snatching the opportunity, I thought, to take her leave of me. They bade us goodnight and set off.

Bruce had been silent up to this point. "Fancy a coffee or a brandy?" he asked.

"Actually, I think an early night might not be such a bad idea," I said, suddenly realizing just how weary I was.

"Yes," he agreed. "It has been a long and eventful day." He helped me to my feet and we set off toward our cabin.

# CHAPTER TWELVE

As we approached our quarters, I could feel the train slowing down and I mentioned this.

"Oh yes," Bruce explained, "The train stables in a siding for the night and therefore passengers can be assured of a good night's rest."

I'd never heard of such a thing but after thinking about it decided it was probably a fortunate thing. I had no idea how well I would be able to sleep in a small bed on a moving train. The passageway of the sleeping coach was now dimly lit. It was quiet except for the noises made by the movement of the slowing train. Bruce and I quickly took turns preparing for bed. I fell asleep quickly but awakened some time later. I glanced at the clock on the desk and realized I had only been sleeping around three hours. I became aware of noises in the next cabin, the one belonging to Nora and Edward, and wondered what its occupants could be doing at this hour. The noises were muffled at first, growing more frequent and more intense. I became fearful and called out to Bruce.

"Bruce," I said softly at first and then louder, "Bruce!"

At that moment there was a scream from the next

cabin. Bruce flew out of bed and flung open the door. Several people were standing in their doorways, obviously also awakened by the commotion. The door to Nora and Edward's cabin was open. Bruce crept toward it cautiously. Suddenly the cabin light went on and Bruce stopped in his tracks. Nora appeared in the doorway. There was blood on her nightgown.

"Nora!" Bruce exclaimed, as he rushed to her side.

"Oh Nora," I said, starting toward her and Bruce.

"It's Edward," she said, quite calmly. I didn't know how she could be so calm. The sight of her was making me quite upset.

"No, Leigh!" Bruce exclaimed, ordering me, "Don't come near here." He was standing next to Nora and looking from me to the scene inside the cabin. "Charles, take her back to your room and wait there." I turned to see Charles standing behind me. A look which I could not read passed between the two men. Nora just stood there silently. Charles began to usher me down the corridor. The conductor had been summoned and was now making his way toward Nora and Bruce. I kept looking back over my shoulder at them until I could no longer see them.

Charles' room was at the opposite end of the car from ours. He opened the door and allowed me to enter first. Once inside, he closed and locked the door. I must have looked startled.

"It's just a precaution, Leigh," he said quietly.

"A precaution against what?" I demanded.

He didn't answer me and went toward the desk. He filled an electric pot with water and switched it on, preparing to make tea. He busied himself making the cups and the cream and sugar ready. I sat there quietly watching him. Although a dozen questions were running through my mind I sensed it would prove futile to ask him anything and anyway, at that moment, I was too tired to try to get answers out of him. He served our tea and we sat in silence drinking it. He had insisted that I take the bed, as I might want to lie down afterward. He sat in the chair by the desk. Although it was quiet in the room, we could hear many sounds outside the tiny cabin – sirens, people moving in the passageway, people talking.

"Why don't you try to rest now, Leigh," Charles said eventually. "This will be a long night."

"Yes, I think I will if you don't mind Charles," I answered wearily.

"Please, go ahead," he replied, "I will be right here."

He was such a gentleman I thought, much like Bruce and despite his and Bruce's strange comings and goings and my many unanswered questions, I instinctively felt safe with him. Again I found myself refusing to believe that they could be tied in to the London 'Creeper' business.

"Where do you suppose we are?" I asked, lying down on top of the bed.

"I have made this journey with Mr. Spenceworth before," he answered, "The train stables in North Berwick for the night."

"Charles, do you think Bruce and Nora are all right? What could have happened in that cabin?" I asked.

He approached the bed, picking up a spare blanket on the way. He unfolded it and covered me with it.

"Just rest," he said, "We'll have news soon enough."

"Thank you Charles," I answered, as I settled onto the pillow. Despite the mayhem going on around me, I couldn't stop myself from drifting off to sleep.

Sometime later I was gently awakened. Bruce was sitting next to me on the bed.

"Oh Bruce," I exclaimed, half sitting up. "What's happened?"

"Edward has been killed," he said quietly, "Their wall safe was robbed and the police think he fought back against the thief."

"Oh my God!" I uttered, "Dead? But how…but who…where is Nora?"

"She is still speaking with the local authorities," he answered, "She was not harmed. The police are conducting interviews with passengers and staff but the conclusion seems to be that whoever did this has already exited the train."

As he spoke I realized that Charles was no longer in the room and I inquired after him.

"He has gone to be with Nora and to give his statement," Bruce said.

"Shall I be required to give one as well?" I asked.

"No," he replied, "We thought it best that you be excused from tedious questioning due to your condition. I was able to recount what we heard and that seemed to satisfy the investigators."

I wondered who "we" was and decided it was probably he and Nora.

There was a knock at the door. Bruce called out before opening the door and Charles answered. Bruce let him in.

"The passengers in this coach have been given the all clear to return to their cabins," Charles announced.

As I moved to get up, I caught sight of the desk clock. It read 3:20.

"Is that really the time?" I asked.

"Yes, I'm afraid so," replied Bruce. "It is very early in the morning.

Bruce took my hand and helped me up.

"Thank you for everything Charles," I said, as I straightened myself up.

He merely smiled and made a slight bow in my direction.

Bruce put his hand on Charles' shoulder as we made our way toward the door. Neither man actually spoke but there had definitely been some unspoken communication passing between them. Bruce and I made our way slowly along the passageway. It was dark outside but I could see all sorts of official vehicles parked alongside the train with lights going and people standing around. Suddenly I caught sight of the stretcher containing the occupied body bag. I must have made some noise because Bruce came closer to me and I turned and buried my head in his shoulder. He held me for several minutes before ushering me the rest of the way to our cabin.

"Can you sleep?" he asked.

"I'm not sure," I answered. "I think…" The rest of what I was going to say was cut short by a knock at the door.

"Who's there?" Bruce called.

"It's Nora," came the answer.

I jumped up from the bed and flung open the door. Nora was standing there and she smiled when she saw me. She was no longer wearing the bloody nightgown.

"Oh Nora!" I exclaimed and I moved to embrace her.

Eventually I released her and she came in and sat down on the desk chair that Bruce offered her. He and I sat down on his bed.

"I'm sorry about all this Leigh," she apologized, "We've certainly spoiled your honeymoon trip."

I stared at her. "You have nothing to be sorry for. I'm the one who's sorry," I said, "I can't believe what you've had to go through. I can't imagine what you've seen."

"Yes," she replied quietly, "Well, look, it's late and I don't think I will go into any details now. We'll have to cancel Edinburgh. I'll be accompanying Edward's body back to London. I wanted to see you before I left."

"You're leaving right away?" I asked. "You shouldn't do this by yourself. Let us come with you," I pleaded, looking at Bruce for his agreement.

"No, darling," she replied, "I'll take care of everything."

"Yes," Bruce said, "Nora is right. The most important thing now is for us to return home. We'll take the train into Edinburgh and arrange to have the helicopter meet us at the airport."

"What about the business you were coming to take care of?" I asked.

"There is nothing more important right now than dealing with this matter," he responded.

The whole business had been understandably exhausting and Bruce and Nora were certainly looking fatigued. I caught a hint of something else in the air, something very intense. I could feel it radiating off them. We said our goodbyes to Nora and reluctantly, at least on my part, sent her off. While Bruce made telephone calls, I stretched out on my bed with the thoughts of just resting but fell fast asleep.

# CHAPTER THIRTEEN

**Bruce woke me** when we arrived at Waverly Station in Edinbugh. From there we motored straight to airport where the helicopter was waiting for us. Much of this time moving from one place to another passed in silence and I was numb to any of the sights we passed. Bruce and Charles looked troubled and preoccupied and I was still, I think, trying to process what had happened.

I had taken the previous chopper ride at night. It was now broad daylight and despite the wave of anxiety we found ourselves engulfed in, I was enjoying the view of the Scottish and English countryside from the air – it was magnificent.

We were very close to Brookside when the craft suddenly gave a lurch, followed by a sputtering sound from the engine. As the pilot cautioned us to brace for a possible impact, Bruce unbuckled his lap belt and came to kneel down beside me. No one uttered a word. Miraculously, the pilot maintained control and set the craft down with only a hard thud. Rob and Elizabeth Major, who had been watching our arrival, as well as the two gardeners who were working nearby, came running over.

"Is everyone all right?" Mrs. Major inquired.

"Leigh? Darling, are you hurt?" Bruce cried.

"I..no..I'm all right. I'm just shaken" I answered.

"I'll summon the authorities, Mr. Spenceworth" said Charles.

"Yes, please see to that immediately," replied Bruce, "John, what the devil happened?" he inquired of the pilot.

"Can't understand it, sir," the man answered, "The chopper had a routine maintenance check the day before we left, and there wasn't a single indication on the first leg of the journey that anything was wrong. Fortunately for us the problem surfaced just as we were preparing to land. Any second sooner, and…well…I'll begin a check on the engine."

"Do, and when you've finished, report to me immediately," ordered Bruce.

Charles had returned from inside to inform Bruce that the proper authorities had been notified and that someone would be sent to assist in the investigation.

We had arrived on the lawn just before noon. Now as soon as we'd cleared the aircraft, Rob came running forward. He embraced his father and then me.

"I'm so happy to see you, are you all right?" he exclaimed.

"And I you, and yes I feel fine," I returned, hugging him tightly. "Come," I continued, trying to lift the mood, "Tell me everything you've been up to," I said taking his hand and walking toward the house. I left the men behind talking amongst themselves. I was trying not to let my imagination run wild, but after all this had been the second accident I had been involved in during one week. Rob talked nonstop about the goings on in the household during our absence and then inquired about our trip.

"Oh it was fascinating," I said, "I have never stayed in a castle. Tell me, Rob, have you had the chance to visit there?"

"Oh yes," he answered, "Father has taken me several times. We've a very tasty lunch prepared for you Leigh," he said as he led me into the breakfast room. The room did look festive. The table was set with fine china and linens with a large floral arrangement at center.

"My goodness, this looks beautiful. But what is the special occasion?" I asked.

"You're homecoming," he answered, "And a celebration because now you'll be with us forever."

"Indeed cause for celebration," remarked Bruce from behind us. I hadn't heard him come in. Rob was gazing happily from one to the other of us so I mustered a smile and took a seat. As Charles and Mrs. Major began serving Bruce said, "We have been invited to attend a party being given in our honor tonight at the home of Patrick and Catherine Ferguson. Patrick, you may recall, is my attorney."

I was taken by surprise because I'd imagined that he would head straight for the office to deal with his pressing business matters in addition to following up the investigation of the helicopter's mysterious mechanical problems. And there was also the matter of following up with Nora to see what assistance, if any, she needed with the arrangements for Edward. He must have sensed my confusion.

"I must go to the office this afternoon and check in with Nora," he said, "But I shall return in ample time for us to attend the party. I wouldn't think of disappointing the Fergusons, that is, unless you are feeling poorly as a result of our unexpected jolt this morning."

"I…yes, of course we'll attend," I agreed, hardly knowing what else to say. I was beginning to realize that a great deal more than I knew was going on. However, at that moment I said nothing as Rob was present.

"Wow!" exclaimed Rob, "A party just for you. Leigh, you should wear your hair up like you did before."

"That is an excellent suggestion Rob," I replied, regaining my composure.

"Hey, maybe the 'Creeper' will…"

"That will do, young man," said Bruce, cutting in rather sternly, "Perhaps you should be getting on with your music lesson."

"Yes sir," answered Rob, getting up to make his departure.

"Rob, may I have one more hug before you go?" I inquired.

"Sure" he said happily. He came over to where I was seated and embraced me. "I really am glad you're home."

"I'm really glad to be back, and I'm especially glad to see you," I returned. Smiling, he left the room.

"Will you need to go to town in preparation for this evening?" Bruce asked.

"No, thank you," I answered.

"Very well, I must be off," he said. He rose and came around to me. After placing a quick kiss on my cheek he looked directly into my eyes. He said nothing, however, and took his leave.

I sat there in deep contemplation over the morning's events. I was reading such conflicting signals from

Bruce. I did believe he truly had feelings for me, but I also felt there was something he was trying to communicate to me. Whatever it was I wished he would just verbalize it and be done with it. Elizabeth Major entered to finish clearing. I presumed Charles had accompanied Bruce. I hastily decided to question the woman about the comments she had made regarding Bruce's first wife.

"Mrs. Major, what did you mean about 'seeing' Mrs. Spenceworth?" I asked bluntly.

The question must have stunned her for she didn't answer right away.

"I didn't mean to speak out of turn Leigh," she said.

"You didn't. I was wondering how you knew I had seen her, and I am curious to know what your experiences with her have been," I said.

She stood there looking at me and then came over to the table and sat down beside me.

"Been seeing her for years," she started, "Began almost right after she passed. At first I'd had the feeling that she'd unfinished business. But, as time passed, I see she is a guardian. She keeps watch over her family. I just noticed the way you stare at her picture and I knew you had seen her."

"Have you ever spoken to her, or she to you?" I asked.

"Oh no ma'am," she answered, looking at me intently.

"What is her name, Mrs. Major?" I inquired.

"Robyn, ma'am," she said.

"Thank you very much for speaking with me Mrs. Major," I said, "Perhaps we can do this again."

"Oh yes, Leigh, anytime you wish," she replied.

I rose then, deciding to retire to my room and begin preparations for that evening.

"I've seen to your things Leigh," she called after me. I turned back to ask what she meant, but she continued, "I've moved your things into the master suite and Mr. Spenceworth's into the dressing room just as he ordered." She, like Mrs. Arnold before her, showed no sign that the arrangement was unusual.

So it was to be a copy of our wedding night, but on a permanent basis. The thought that we would be in such close proximity was somewhat disconcerting, but I merely thanked Mrs. Major and took my leave. I had never seen the master suite and now would conduct my own tour. As I crossed the foyer to climb the stairs I heard Mrs. Major's voice behind me.

"Leigh, Miss Nora is on the telephone for you," she called, "You can pick up the extension there." I headed for the device sitting on a small table just outside Bruce's study.

"Nora?"

"Leigh, darling," she said, "Are you all right?"

"Am I all right?" I echoed, "I should be asking that of you. After what you've been through…"

"Please don't worry about me," she replied, sounding very much like her normal self, "I'm fine. I've seen to the arrangements and notified what family Edward had left. I've already told Bruce there will be a very small and private ceremony tomorrow. That is the way the family wants it."

"Surely you and Bruce will be allowed to attend, you were both close to him," I said.

"It will be family only," she answered, "I have already said my goodbyes and I know Bruce will be in contact with the family."

"Are you certain there is nothing that we can do?"

I asked, reflecting on the arrangements. I found her extremely calm demeanor suspicious, after all she had witnessed what had happened in that cabin and yet her tone of voice suggested that the handling of it all was just a matter of routine.

"I've got to run now, love, but I'll stop over tomorrow. Bye for now," she said and rang off.

She was strong-willed, I'd give her that and it would indeed be wonderful to see her. I climbed the great staircase, pausing on the landing beneath Robyn Spenceworth's portrait. Although I stood for several minutes studying it, nothing unusual happened. I pressed on toward the master suite. I opened the door and stepped inside. I came face to face with a huge canopy bed neatly situated under a large stained glass window, which featured the family coat of arms. The window was just one of the many striking features of the façade of the house so I was able to get my bearings as to where the room lay in the scheme of things. Next to the bed on either side was a nightstand, upon which stood a vase filled with long stemmed yellow roses, my favorite flower.

As my eyes traveled around the room I noticed it had its own bath and a separate dressing room. I stole a peek at the latter and found that, like at the castle, a bed had been made up for Bruce. I crossed the room to glance at the bath and found it equally as luxurious as the one down the hall. The shower had stained glass doors, which also featured the coat of arms, and the room also contained a marble tub. Scattered around the room were smaller vases containing yellow roses. I wondered whose idea it had been to place them there. The evening gown I had worn several nights before was hanging from the door, and my toiletries had been neatly placed on the vanity. Mrs. Major had certainly thought of everything.

At that moment there was a knock on the door.

"Come in," I called.

Mrs. Major appeared. "I hope everything is all right."

"You have outdone yourself Mrs. Major," I answered, "The room looks lovely and I want to thank you for bringing in my belongings and my gown for tonight. Yellow roses are my favorite, how did you know?"

"Mr. Spenceworth ordered the flowers. I've come to say I'd be happy to help with your hair," she offered.

"That would wonderful," I replied, "And then I think I'll have a soak in the tub before I dress."

I sat down at the dressing table and together we managed to pile my hair atop my head in a rather attractive style. Then Mrs. Major drew my bath and left me. I enjoyed a leisurely soak, dressed and made my way to my former room to retrieve the jewels Bruce had given me. As I was working the wall safe's combination, I heard a sound behind me. I whirled around to find my specter standing before me.

"Robyn! What is going on?" I asked, "Why are you…" Suddenly the door opened. She vanished instantly and Bruce walked in. He surveyed the room as if expecting to find someone else there.

"I came to retrieve this," I said, showing him the velvet case.

"Let me help you," he offered, and he crossed the room and took the case from me. He lifted the lid and took the necklace into his hands. "Turn around," he commanded. As I did so, he stepped very close to me and placed the gem around my neck. He moved even closer and put his arms around me. We stood silently, looking at our reflection in the mirror just as we had done on our ill-fated train journey. I was most definitely affected by his closeness and I wanted very desperately to speak frankly with him. He seemed extraordinarily preoccupied. We were interrupted as Rob came rushing in.

"Wow, you two look great," he said.

We flew apart and despite the tensions between us, Bruce and I smiled at each other and then at Rob.

"Leigh, you look like a princess," he exclaimed.

"And I feel like one too," I confessed, fumbling to secure my earrings to my ear lobes.

"Rob, why don't you accompany us downstairs?" Bruce suggested. As we left the room, Rob linked arms with each of us. Downstairs in the foyer he assisted me with my wrap and bade us goodnight.

# CHAPTER FOURTEEN

CHARLES WAS WAITING just outside the door with the car. The sun was sinking as we set off. As we motored along, Bruce explained that the Fergusons lived several towns over, in Manchester.

"This evening will provide an excellent opportunity for you to meet many of the board members as well as many prominent members of London society," he continued, "It is very important that we…you and I must present a unified front."

It was a strange choice of words but he was obviously sending me a message. Abruptly, I recalled Robyn Spenceworth's previous advice to me, "Trust in Bruce."

"I realize that we have been through a great deal in a short period of time. I…" he started. He was searching for words, something I had seldom seen him do.

Obeying my instincts to trust him I said, "I understand." He looked at me intently then. I returned his gaze. It was as if we were on the verge of some breakthrough communication. The car came to a stop, signaling our arrival at the Ferguson house. As Charles opened the door, the moment was lost. Now it was show time. Charles remained with the car while we made our way to the door. It opened before Bruce had a chance to ring the bell.

"Bruce, old man," said Patrick as he greeted us and shook hands with Bruce. He stepped forward and embraced me and then presented his wife, Catherine.

"Congratulations my dears," she said, "We are so pleased to have you," she continued as they ushered us into the front hall.

"We are honored," I answered linking arms with Bruce, more for moral support than as a show of solidarity, although it played nicely into the plan of presenting a unified front. We remained inseparable for at least an hour. Our hosts skillfully maneuvered us about the room presenting us, mostly me, to this group and that. Bruce was obviously well known to everyone and worked the room with tremendous sophistication. I wondered what impressions people were forming about me and about us as a couple.

The Fergusons had had the party catered and servants were constantly weaving in and out with food and drink. Guests enjoyed one classical piece of music after another from a solitary pianist seated at a grand piano. I overheard several men mentioning "poor Edward" and "that awful business on the train" and for the first time since Edward's death I realized that Bruce and I were meant to be in that train cabin, not Edward. One or the other of us could have been killed. The thought upset me very much, not only the part that it could have been us, but the guilt that Edward was in the wrong place at the wrong time because of his kind deed of trading cabins with us. I wondered if Bruce was having similar thoughts.

Gradually, Mrs. Ferguson lured me away from the men and I sipped coffee with her and a select group of women. I found my hostess to be a truly charming woman and I hoped that I would have the opportunity to come to know her better. Eventually I excused myself and went in search of the lavatory. I had been directed to the second floor but apparently had not listened carefully enough for once there, I was not sure which door to choose. I picked one and turned the knob. I had only opened the door slightly when I realized I had selected a study, not the bathroom. As I prepared to retreat a sound caught my attention. I stepped further inside the room and found Bruce, robbing the wall safe. I gasped.

"Leigh…" he began.

I had not shut the door and now could hear our hostess and other guests headed in our direction. I quickly stepped out of the room and closed the door. Just then Mrs. Ferguson appeared followed by several people for whom she was obviously conducting a tour. Although shocked by what I just seen, I did not want Bruce discovered.

"Ashleigh, what is it?" my hostess was saying.

"Catherine, I…I'm so sorry," I stuttered, "I am not feeling well." Although I was trying to think fast, this was not far from the truth. "Perhaps you could help me downstairs, I'd like to find Bruce."

"Of course, my dear," she answered. She and the others gathered around me and gingerly ushered me to the first floor. I must have looked ill for as we made our way through the crowd people stopped and stared. All at once I saw Bruce chatting with several other men. I wondered how he had finished his work and returned to the party so quickly. As soon as he saw me he quickly came over to us.

"Darling, are you all right?"

I could hardly look him in the eye. "I'm so sorry, I'm not feeling well," I managed.

"Catherine, I believe I had better take her home. Perhaps we have overdone it a bit what with all of the events of the last couple of days," he offered, "Please accept my apology and our sincere thanks for a magnificent evening."

The man certainly had my nomination for an Oscar winning performance – one minute he was burglarizing the house and the next showering his gratitude upon its mistress. I truly felt ill. Bruce took my arm and guided me through the crowd making our goodbyes along the way. Outside I saw that Charles already had the car door open and the engine running. I hesitated momentarily before climbing in, but did so and took the seat opposite Bruce instead of next to him. The car started off. I waited for him to say something and when he didn't, I couldn't contain myself.

"What the hell is going on?" I demanded.

"Leigh, I realize how this must look. Please allow me to explain…"

He was denied the opportunity as Charles had suddenly slammed on the brakes. As the car stopped Bruce opened the door and jumped out. I looked out the window and saw that we had barely reached the end of the Ferguson's driveway, but now another vehicle blocked our path. I started to climb out when Bruce shoved me back and shut the door screaming, "Charles, get her out of here." Without uttering a word, Charles threw the automobile into reverse and started backing up the drive toward the house. Although it was dark, our headlights shone on Bruce being forced into the car that had blocked our path. Charles parked in front of the house and with me in tow, rang the bell. Mrs. Ferguson answered the door and looked from one to the other of us.

Charles said, "May I use your telephone, Madame? Mr. Spenceworth has just been kidnapped."

Word of the kidnapping spread through the room like a wildfire. Charles escorted me to a chair and then followed Catherine Ferguson into another room where he could make calls privately. I sat there, I am sure, in a state of shock. I thought back on how the week had started with my hopeful journey to a new country and had ended with a pregnancy, a marriage, a death, my discovery that my new husband was a burglar and now a kidnapping. I was beginning to wish I would wake up from a bad dream. The Fergusons and several of the women had gathered around me and were offering words of consolation and support. Charles re-entered the room and came directly over to where I was seated.

"A car is being sent for us Mrs. Spenceworth," he reported, "We are to go directly to Brookside."

I said nothing, but nodded my head. Some time later the car arrived. Charles helped me to the door where I paused to thank my hosts.

"Patrick, Catherine…thank you so much, for everything," I said. They embraced me and made me promise to phone them with any news. Outside, Charles held the rear door of the car open for me. I climbed in and to my surprise, found myself sitting across from Nora.

"Nora!" I exclaimed, "What on Earth are you doing here? How did you…do you know about Bruce?"

"Yes, I know," she said quietly, "Look, we've a great deal to talk about and you've had a tremendous shock. I want you to sit calmly until we reach Brookside."

Charles had climbed in and taken a seat next to me. I looked from one to the other. I merely nodded my head and sat back. The ride back to the house passed in complete silence.

# CHAPTER FIFTEEN

It was late when we arrived, and it was obvious that all members of the household had gone to bed. The car left us off at the front door but did not leave. Charles and Nora escorted me inside and straight into Bruce's study. Once inside Nora went straight to the stone cherub, pressing it and opening the secret entrance to the tunnel. Although I gasped, she and Charles said nothing. They led me through the entryway and along the passage until we reached the wooden door. Nora opened it, and then entered a code using the keypad. Within seconds the metal door flew open to reveal a room that, to me, looked like some kind of intelligence command post. There were computers, phones, maps, desks, files. Nora took me by the hand and led me through the room to the rear, where we passed through another doorway leading to a small office. Charles had followed us and had seated himself on one of the available chairs. Nora indicated that I should do the same. Once I was seated, she began speaking.

"Leigh, there is a great deal I must tell you and I am going to be direct. The events of this evening have forced me to do so earlier than we had planned. Bruce and I work for MI5 and we are involved…"

"What?!" I gasped, interrupting her, "What are you saying?"

"I am saying that we work for the United Kingdom's security intelligence agency."

I sat there staring at her, trying to digest the news that my best friend and my husband were spies.

"We are involved in an investigation that has been ongoing for a few years and that spans several continents," she continued, "We believe that Edward's death and Bruce's abduction tonight are directly related to this investigation."

"The incident on the train wasn't a burglary?" I asked.

"No," she answered.

"You don't own an employment agency?" I asked bewildered.

"The agency is real, but exists as a cover and as a means to place our people in strategic positions," she replied.

"How long have you been involved with…this?" I demanded.

"I was recruited shortly after we graduated from college," she answered.

"All these years…." I said, "I never had any idea."

"You weren't supposed to," she said.

"Am I allowed to ask what it is that you are working on?" I inquired. A look passed between her and Charles that I could not read.

"Leigh, there is more…and…this is not going to be easy for you to hear," she continued, "We are trying to crack an international smuggling ring that has been using, among many other avenues, Spenceworth's as a means of legitimately getting stolen items smuggled to buyers in other countries. When we learned about Spenceworth's, we approached Bruce. He came on board to avenge the family reputation. This secret room has been invaluable in providing us the privacy we needed to research and plan. We have had numerous operatives working in many countries, and we have had the assistance of many private citizens." She paused here and I could feel my stomach beginning to churn. "Jack was one such private citizen. He was using his professional contacts to run down several leads for us. He had provided us with critical information just before…we are…we are certain his death was not an accident. I am so sorry Leigh," she finished.

I shut my eyes, fighting back the tears, but they came anyway. It was horrifying to know that I had lost Jack, and my son, to some sinister plot. My mind was racing and suddenly several things became clear, like why Nora had come so quickly after Jack had been killed and why Bruce wanted to marry me.

Nora had said nothing as if giving me some time to process what she had said. Now she said quietly, "Leigh, your life is in danger. You are not to go anywhere without Charles or one of our agents by your side."

"So, Charles can add one more skill to his resume. Chauffer, manservant and spy," I said dryly.

Charles said nothing, but made a slight nod in my direction.

"Seriously," Nora continued, "You have had three misses. Obviously they think Jack or Bruce may have told you something…"

"Three misses? What do you mean? I…oh, you

mean the accident in the warehouse and the trouble with the helicopter?" I guessed. "What's the third?"

"Edward and I were in your cabin….." she said quietly.

"Oh my God!" I said, really grasping that Edward's death had not been due to some random burglary, but rather to a coldly calculated plan of attack that had been meant for me.

"You see what I mean?" she asked, "Now we've got to get back as I've sent for Dr. Thompson. This evening has been a tremendous shock. I want him to look you over and then you're to go to bed." We had all risen and had begun to make our way back to the house. "I want you to stay close to the house for the next couple of days…"

"Close to the house?" I said angrily, "If you think I'm going to sit back and do nothing you're mistaken. They've killed one husband and kidnapped another, not to mention murdering my child." Tears streamed down my face. "I'm in, whether you like it or not."

"Leigh that is ridiculous. You haven't had the proper training and you are presently in no condition to take anything of this magnitude on. You are over your head…"

"You've heard of on-the-job training I presume," I continued sarcastically, "Well, teacher, get out your books." I was wild with fury and totally out of control.

We had reached Bruce's study and the secret door had closed behind us. Nora opened the study door and we entered the foyer just in time to hear the front bell. Charles admitted Dr. Thompson.

Nora regarded me nervously and then whispered to me, "What I've told you tonight must remain between us." I nodded and we moved forward to greet the doctor. He was extremely upset by the news about Bruce. Nora took the opportunity to plant the story that Bruce had most likely been taken to be traded for a considerable ransom as the family was wealthy. The doctor insisted on giving me a potion to relax me and help me to sleep, and I was fighting the idea. Finally he seemed to give in asking for a glass of warm milk for me. Charles went to retrieve it while the doctor excused himself to make a telephone call from the extension just outside the study. Nora and I retreated into the study to sit and wait for the men. Charles came in carrying a glass of milk, followed by the doctor moments later. I obediently drank the milk. As we rose to see the doctor off, I suddenly began to feel weak and dizzy.

"What…what have you done?" I asked, but blacked out before anyone could answer.

# CHAPTER SIXTEEN

It didn't take me long when I awoke to realize that I had been drugged or that I had slept all night and half the next day. I rose, quickly dressed and headed downstairs to see who was about. As I crossed the foyer I heard voices in the drawing room. I entered to find Rob, being comforted by Nora and Charles. Upon seeing me, the boy ran into my arms crying.

"Oh Leigh," he sobbed, "Am I to lose father?"

I looked at Charles and Nora but neither spoke. I held the boy, gently stroking his hair.

"Nothing is going to happen to your father," I said, trying to sound confident, "Please, Rob, I don't want you to worry. We are going to do whatever it takes to get him back."

Charles had risen and come over to where we were standing. He took Rob's hand and led him from the room. I turned to Nora.

"So, what is the game plan?" I inquired.

"At this point, we wait. Undoubtedly they will make contact," she answered.

"Who is 'they'? You must know who is behind this? Why hasn't contact been made already?" I demanded.

She hesitated but then said, "Yes, most of the operatives are known to us. We were just about to start picking up those based in London when Bruce was taken. Obviously, there is a leak."

"Who is involved at Spenceworth's?" I asked.

"Leigh, I would prefer not to get into this with you. The less you know the safer you are. You will be on a need-to-know basis only. That way you are less of a target. You are to stay close to the house and try to carry on," she said.

"You must be joking," I said angrily, "I am as involved as anyone and I demand to know…" I was interrupted by Charles who advised us that Marco Abruzzi was at the front door asking to see me. I looked at Nora.

"Yes," she nodded, "See him. I am going to slip out of the room, but I will be close by."

I stood waiting to receive my guest. Charles led him in, announced him and withdrew.

"My dear," he said as he came over and took my hands, "I am so sorry about this business. It is dreadful, what with you barely back from your wedding trip."

"Thank you Mr. Abruzzi for your concern," I replied, seating myself and trying to remain cool. "It was kind of you to make the trip all the way out here. How are things at the office?"

"Running smoothly, nothing for you to concern yourself with," he answered, strolling slowly around the room. "In fact, I would remain as uninvolved as possible if I were you." He had said it quietly, but I knew there was something behind the words.

"What do you mean?" I asked bluntly.

"Such a shame about the loss of your first husband," he went on, "And a child too, I believe. And now Edward……But you can't say I didn't try to warn you," he said, looking very pleased with himself, "Oh yes, the anonymous phone caller warning you to leave was me. I couldn't resist the chance to play with you. Of course I really can't allow you to go anywhere."

I stared at him. There was evil emanating from his very being. I stood up.

"You…it's you…" I gasped, "You had my family killed. You son of a bitch…"

He laughed quietly.

"Where is Bruce?" I demanded.

"Where are the items that were taken from the Ferguson household?" he demanded, ignoring my inquiry about Bruce. He had stopped moving about the room and stood facing me.

"I…I'm not sure," I said, playing for time.

"I will call you this afternoon at precisely four o'clock. Perhaps we can arrange a trade." With that he turned and quickly left the room. Almost immediately Nora came in.

"Nora, he…" I started but the words wouldn't come. I sank down in a chair, shaking violently.

"I know Leigh," she answered. She sat next to me and put her arm around me. "I heard it all. We have known he was a major player for quite some time and we suspected he had a role in ordering Jack's death. The items he was talking about are the ones you saw Bruce taking from the Ferguson wall safe."

"So, I really am married to London's 'Creeper'," I said.

"Well, yes and no," Nora continued, "Bruce was

playing a role, anonymously or so we thought, in order to flush Marco and his confederates out. And a damn good job he's done. Brookside was to be next on the hit list in order to keep appearances up and avert any suspicion from Bruce, if anyone was suspicious of Bruce. We've identified nearly the entire ring thanks to him and Jack and numerous operatives in the field. As I said last night, this thing spans several continents although we are convinced the master mind is here."

"So what happens at four o'clock?" I asked, "Abruzzi will be expecting to talk with me."

"Mmm…yes, it would seem as though we may need your assistance," she agreed reluctantly. "Listen, I'm going to talk to Charles and then report in on this latest development. We'll talk again later."

I could hardly believe that I had stood face to face with the man who had very possibly ordered my family's murder. Instead of sadness I found myself filled with rage. There was no way I would sit this one out on the sidelines. I was more determined than ever to rescue Bruce. As I sat there it suddenly occurred to me what Bruce had meant by "avenging" our households.

While I was no intelligence mastermind, I knew that Bruce was probably still in England. The question was, where? How could I hope to find him before he was harmed? After all, the country's finest were on the job. All at once I thought of Robyn Spenceworth. It had been days since I'd seen her and she previously appeared when she wanted me to discover something. I wondered how one went about contacting a ghost. I decided to go out into the garden where she had first appeared to me. I informed Mrs. Major that I would be in the garden and proceeded to walk some distance before sitting on one of the benches.

"Robyn, please," I pleaded aloud, "Please, you know what is happening. If you can help me…please show me." I waited and watched. The afternoon was waning away. I closed my eyes wondering what I was doing. When I opened them, she stood before me. I got up without saying a word. She motioned for me to follow, which I did without reservation. She was heading straight for the house. She was some distance ahead of me when I saw her vanish through a wall.

"Robyn, wait!" I called in frustration. Obviously I could not follow her through the wall. I racked my brain trying to grasp the meaning of what she'd done. I looked at the house and then tried to visualize a floor plan in my mind to help shed light on why she had chosen this spot. Suddenly I remembered that Bruce's study should be on the other side of this wall. I raced inside the house and into the room. I surveyed it, looking for some clue to what she was trying to tell me. I noticed papers lying on Bruce's desk and went closer to inspect them. To my surprise they were the schematics for Spenceworth's, with the layout of the cellars on the top of the pile. I had toured the partially subterranean first floor with Charles and probably had assumed that it was the basement, the lowest level, but the drawing in front of me seemed to indicate otherwise. Immediately I realized there must be true cellars beneath. So, they had hidden Bruce right under our noses and had undoubtedly used the space to house the smuggled items. What a setup. "Thank you, Robyn," I called out. I bundled up the drawing and went in search of Nora and Charles.

# CHAPTER SEVENTEEN

**I found them** in the drawing room.

"I know where Bruce is," I stated bluntly, unfolding the diagram. They looked at me in disbelief and then at the picture I laid out before them.

"Where did you get this?" Nora demanded, "I have never seen this, have you Charles?"

"I was vaguely aware that cellars exist below the first floor but I had thought them completely sealed off," Charles answered.

I was not about to reveal my source. I said, "Look, where this came from is unimportant at the moment. What does matter is that we can plan a rescue. Look, when Abruzzi calls back I can agree to meet him across town while you lead the rescue operation."

"You will do no such thing!" said Nora hotly.

"Either you two work with me or I go alone," I said, giving them an ultimatum.

They looked at each other and then at me. "Yes, all right," said Nora nodding her head, "There may be something in this and anyhow we need to keep close tabs on you," she scowled at me. "Charles, suppose you and Leigh go in search of Bruce. If you're spotted in Spenceworth's no one will think twice, you can make up a story about why you're there. I'll pose as Leigh and meet Marco with the cavalry standing by. It's about time we picked him up. Leigh, you and Charles will have to slip out through the tunnel and make your way through the fields to the road. Satisfied?"

I looked at her and smiled saying, "This reminds me of our college days when you used to help me research my stories. We did some fantastic things to get at the truth." She smiled and took my hand. I continued, "Nora, do you think Bruce…I mean, will he…will they…" I couldn't finish.

"Hey," she answered, "We will find him, don't you worry. Look, I've got to call the office before Abruzzi calls. We have got to set this plan in motion. Honestly Leigh, please try not to worry. Everything is going to come right."

She and Charles excused themselves and I sat mulling over the situation. I was amazed and impressed by Nora. She was calm and level headed, even in the face of extreme danger. To think that she had been working as an agent all these years and had been able to disguise it from me simply astounded me. Obviously my powers of observation were not so keen or she was truly a master of deception. True, she did work abroad which helped keep me in the dark, but what of my own husband, Jack? He had been involved in providing intelligence and I never even suspected. Nora had said the less I knew, the better. Jack must have believed the same thing, or was instructed to keep me in the dark. I didn't have to know everything now to know the stakes were deadly. All at once the telephone sounded. As I stood up, Nora and Charles entered the room.

"Find out where he wants to meet," Nora directed, "Tell him you do have the items from the Ferguson safe."

Charles had picked up the receiver. "Spenceworth residence, may I help you?" he inquired. "One moment sir," he continued and then nodded to me. I put the instrument to my ear.

"Hello?"

"Are you in a position to make a trade?" asked Marco.

"Yes," I answered.

"Be at the National Gallery at ten in the morning on Wednesday," he ordered.

"The National Gallery on Wednesday at ten," I repeated. Nora nodded her head. "I will be there."

"Come alone," he said.

"Yes, I will come alone," I answered, "Is Bruce all right? Can I speak with…" He had terminated the connection. "Why on Earth are we waiting until Wednesday? Why isn't he doing this now?" I demanded.

Nora sat quietly, thinking. "I don't know," she started, "I have to leave for awhile. I'll check in and see if we got anything from that call – we have a trace on the phone. Leigh, stay in the house. Charles will be here to look after you and there are men around the perimeter."

When she had gone I spent some time with Rob. The child was devastated but putting up a good front. I read to him from a favorite book, helped him with his bath and sat with him while he ate his supper. After I had tucked him in for the night, I retired to my own room. Elizabeth Major had left a sandwich and a glass of milk on a tray. As I ate I paced back and forth restlessly. Marco was desperate to get his hands on the merchandise as he undoubtedly had buyers waiting, so why delay our meeting? Why not meet now? Something did not feel right. From somewhere nearby I heard the words, "Bruce is in danger."

"Robyn?" I called out. She did not appear. The warning was repeated, "Bruce is in danger."

I left my room and ran down the stairs, calling out "Charles, Charles!" as I went. He met me in the foyer.

"Charles, Bruce is in danger. We've got to go for him now," I cried breathlessly.

He didn't ask how or why, he went to the telephone extension outside Bruce's study and placed a call.

"Nora Blaisedale, please," he said. Several seconds passed and then he said, "Please have her ring Brookside immediately. Please advise her it is an emergency."

"Charles?"

"She is indisposed at the moment," he explained.

I wasn't exactly sure what he meant but I knew we didn't have time to wait.

"Can Mrs. Major be trusted?" I asked. He nodded. "Good, then call her as we'll be needing a decoy. She is about the same height as I am. She'll need to put on my coat and hat and take a car into the city. Have her stop at several stores and shop for at least an hour before returning. Then there is the matter of transportation for us." He looked at me as though sizing me up.

"Mr. Spenceworth keeps a car parked off the road in the woods behind the house, in case an emergency exit from the rear should become necessary," Charles said quietly.

"Yes…of course…" I said, "Would you please instruct Mrs. Major and then meet me in the study?"

Charles left to carry out my command and I went into the study to retrieve the schematics for Spenceworth's. I stood looking at them, trying to memorize what led where. Shortly, Charles returned.

"She's off?" I asked. He nodded. I picked up the drawings and moved toward the mantel. I touched the cherub and the secret door swung open. As I started through I glanced back and saw Charles securing a revolver, a box of ammunition and two flashlights from one of the desk drawers. Our eyes met, but neither of us spoke. He quickly followed me into the tunnel. We moved along at a good pace and soon found ourselves climbing the stairs to exit via the door under the altar in the family crypt. At this point Charles took the lead. Although it was dark we made our way through the woods without much difficulty. We walked in silence for quite some time and eventually came upon the car neatly camouflaged.

As Charles maneuvered the roads I said, "From what I can see, the cellars appear to have several possible entries through shafts that connect with the city's sewer system. We should be able to gain access through one of the large run-off drains near the building."

Charles had been silent but now said, "Are you quite certain about this, Leigh?"

"Absolutely certain, Charles," I answered. I sensed he was giving me the option to think twice or back out.

"Very good then," he replied. He was an incredibly loyal man and I was immensely grateful that he possessed the quality. We parked the car some distance from Spenceworth's and made our way on foot. As we neared the building I selected a likely entry point. Charles heaved the lid off the drain and we began our descent into the sewer system. We tried to keep a perspective on where the building lie in comparison to our position and Charles marked the way with torn pieces of paper so we might retrace our steps quickly. We came upon one steel door and then another, but there was no budging them.

I was beginning to think I'd made an error when we came upon a metal door standing ajar. Quietly we sneaked inside. It was dark but there was faint light coming from somewhere ahead of us. We had no real way of knowing if we were under the Spenceworth store or not. As my eyes adjusted to the low light I became aware that the room was filled with cardboard boxes and wooden crates of different sizes and shapes. Very slowly we made our way toward a dim light.

As we got closer to the light, I stopped to examine the contents of a box which was topless – the top was standing propped up against it. I picked up the top and turned it in the direction of the light. It had the Spenceworth logo on it. I brushed aside some packing material with my hand and felt around in the box. My hand came in contact with some type of glassware. I gently lifted the item from the box and saw that it was a porcelain canister. I lifted its lid. Inside were several pieces of jewelry. I held up a piece for Charles to see and then quietly returned the items.

We were far enough into the room at this point to see that there was a door not far from us on the far wall. We pressed on. As we got closer to the door, and the light, we moved more cautiously. Charles motioned for me to stay behind him. As we came out of the maze of boxes, we simultaneously spied a cot to the right of the door near a desk on which sat a weakly lit lamp. There was a body lying on the cot. My heart leaped into my throat and I rushed forward before Charles could stop me. Even though the posterior of the person faced us, I knew it was Bruce. I knelt down next to him, Charles close behind me.

"Bruce…Bruce," I whispered. I gently turned him over and gasped at the sight before me. He had been badly beaten. "Oh my God," I cried, "Bruce…" I gently stroked his hair and face. He opened his eyes then and I was certain he recognized us but he did not have the strength at that moment to say anything.

"Charles, we are going to have to carry him," I stated.

"But, Madam," he protested, "Your condition…"

"I am in perfectly fine condition," I interrupted, "Here, I'll take this side. You take that arm."

Between us we managed to heave Bruce to his feet and had supported his weight with our own bodies when we heard someone coming. The door that we had been heading toward had been left standing ajar. I motioned to Charles to lay Bruce down. We did this quickly, and no doubt uncomfortably for Bruce, and then hid ourselves behind a nearby group of boxes. I was shocked to see Lydia Markham enter the room. She was carrying a tray of food which she set on the desk and then she moved close to the cot to check on Bruce. Charles indicated to me that he was going to make a move. He rushed forward and grabbed the woman from behind. She let out a scream before he could subdue her. I would never have believed that Charles, of all people, would strike a woman, however, he gave Lydia a right hook that sent her reeling. She hit the wall and slumped to the floor, unconscious. Her cry had evidently alarmed her confederates because we could hear the sound of feet moving quickly above us.

"Hurry!" I cried, "They will be here in a minute." We heaved Bruce up and each put one of his arms over a shoulder. We half dragged, half carried him toward our exit. Charles had drawn his revolver and it was a good thing for just as we neared the rear door the shooting began. Charles returned fire as we hurried through the steel door which Charles slammed shut. He shoved something into the lock. Bruce was very groggy but seemed to understand that we were making a break for it and he tried his best to assist in the escape.

It wasn't until we were moving along the sewer that I realized I had been hit. I had taken a bullet to the shoulder but I said nothing to the men. I kept telling myself we must keep going, we must make it to the car. Charles had a good fifteen years on Bruce, but to my amazement when we reached the stairs leading from the sewer up to the street, he hoisted Bruce over his shoulder and climbed up and out of the drain. I had a hard time making it out because of my wound, but Charles reached down and pulled me the rest of the way. It was then that he noticed the blood on my shirt. I shook my head signaling it was not the time to discuss my injury.

We could hear footsteps and voices below us. We gathered up Bruce and made our way toward the car. We were losing momentum with my injury and Bruce's weakened state. As we stood on the corner a bus came and stopped in front of us. On impulse I motioned to Charles who quickly understood my meaning. The three of us boarded the bus. The driver glanced at us and was, not surprisingly, startled by our appearances. He said nothing, however, and we slowly moved down the aisle toward the back. Due to the late hour there were few passengers but they, like the driver, were alarmed by the sight of us. No one spoke. From our seats we could see our pursuers running down the street, apparently unaware that we were motoring past them. The fresh air seemed to revive Bruce for he was able to sit up on his own. He noticed the blood on my shirt.

"Dear God," he exclaimed hoarsely, "Leigh…"

"Please, it's not that bad," I said lying. It hurt like hell and I was beginning to feel nauseous.

"Charles, do we have a car?" he asked, sounding like the old take charge Bruce I knew.

"We've had to abandon it, sir," Charles answered.

"Look, we've got to get to a safe place. She needs a doctor immediately," he cried.

"Help is nearby, sir," Charles replied.

All the while they had been talking our fellow passengers sat mesmerized, staring at us as though watching a television drama unfold before them. Presently Charles rose, and the three of us stumbled to the front of the bus. It stopped and as we exited I noted that we had gotten off at Southwark Bridge. We started forward and I wondered just how far I would be able to make it before I collapsed. To my amazement, instead of walking across the bridge, we left the road and started down the embankment toward the river. Under the bridge, near the water I saw a small community of people. They were shabbily dressed, dirty and many of them were peering at us from under cardboard boxes. Several came forward and greeted Charles by name. I wondered what his connection to these people was. Charles left Bruce and I holding each other up and stood talking with several men. Within seconds he came back followed by two of them.

"Mr. and Mrs. Spenceworth, may I present Donald and Hugh. They will look after you until I return," he announced. As he spoke, he traded jackets and hats with the man he had introduced as Donald.

"Charles…" Bruce started.

"Sir, I am going for help. I don't believe we were followed and it is unlikely that anyone will look for you here. I will return shortly with assistance, with the whole bloody agency if necessary," Charles promised. I had never heard him swear.

"Good man," said Bruce.

"Sir, Madame," he said and then swiftly set off on foot.

"Come on mates," said Donald, "Come closer to the fire. Let's 'ave a proper look at your wounds."

We were assisted by our new found friends. The warmth of the fire felt good.

"Leigh, I'm going to have to look at that shoulder," Bruce declared.

I nodded. I unbuttoned my blouse and he helped me slip it off my shoulder. I cried out as his fingers probed front and then back.

"There is no point of exit," he announced, "This is going to have to come out as soon as possible."

"I'll fetch what ye'll need," offered Donald, "And the Mrs., as she's had training as a doctor's helper, she has."

I was less than thrilled about what they were contemplating, but I was growing weaker and I forced myself to have faith in Bruce. Even I realized that the longer the bullet remained lodged in my shoulder, the greater the chance I had of infection or lead poisoning or both. I knew it had to come out for the baby's sake. Donald returned with a small bag and his wife. She smiled and began taking instruments from the bag. Bruce called for hot water, alcohol and blankets. I marveled at these people who came to our aid as if we were long lost friends instead of strangers. They asked no questions, made no judgments but offered their help unconditionally.

"Darling, everything is going to be all right," Bruce said. I merely nodded, laying down where he had indicated.

"Donald, Hugh," Bruce called. The men knelt down next to me, one on each side, each holding an arm. Bruce gave me something to bite down on. I saw Donald's wife holding the knife she had sterilized in the fire. She handed it to Bruce, who without hesitation plunged his fingers into my wound. I never felt the knife as I blacked out from the excruciating pain.

# CHAPTER EIGHTEEN

I WAS SOMEWHERE, drifting pleasantly. I heard someone calling my name urgently over and over. My eyelids were so heavy it was impossible to lift them. Still I heard voices. I forced myself to open my eyes and found myself looking up at Bruce and Nora.

"Thank God!" Nora exclaimed. As she spoke I became aware of a siren and of the fact that we were mobile. "We are on the way to the hospital Leigh. Just hang on," she begged. I tried to speak but no words would come. I reached out and took her hand. Bruce put his hand over ours. I closed my eyes knowing I was safe and allowed myself to drift away.

When I came to again I was at the hospital, this time looking up at Dr. Thompson and several medical personnel. I heard Nora telling the doctor that I had been delivering the ransom and was caught in the crossfire when the deal went sour. He admonished her quite severely for allowing me to have had any such role in the affair and she took the scolding very humbly, considering I was entirely to blame for my predicament. The doctor and his team gently undressed me and examined my shoulder. Bruce had insisted on remaining by my side while Nora stepped out for an update from her men.

"Fine work, Bruce," the doctor said nodding, "Now Leigh, we are going to try to hear the baby's heartbeat." He applied a warm gel to the lower portion of my abdomen and then placed an instrument on my belly. He moved it slowly and methodically from one side to the other. One could have heard a pin drop in that room. All at once there was a blip followed by a steady stream of them. Tears of joy rolled down my cheeks and I noted that Bruce and Dr. Thompson were wiping their eyes. The doctor went on to order blood tests and an x-ray of my shoulder. I was also to be attached to a fetal monitor for the night and receive antibiotics intravenously to stave off any possible infection from my wound. Bruce was insisting on spending the night with me.

"Have a cot brought in, that'll do," he ordered.

"We'll discuss the sleeping accommodations after we've x-rayed your ribs," the doctor replied, "You took quite a beating young man. I need to be certain nothing is broken."

"There's no need, I'm perfectly fine…" Bruce started.

"I'll decide," interrupted the doctor sternly.

"Very well, Ian," Bruce conceded.

"Nora and I won't let your wife out of our sight until your return," Dr. Thompson said, "Besides, I'm certain these fine gentlemen will handle anything that may arise." The doctor was referring to the army of men, agents I presumed, who had arrived and were hovering around us. He finished cleaning my wound.

"Ashleigh, try to relax," the doctor suggested,

"Bruce should be back in less than one hour. We'll move you to a private room now and get the monitor and intravenous drip in place."

"Thank you Dr. Thompson," I said smiling after him. When he and Bruce had gone, Nora and I were escorted to a room. We remained silent as several nurses attached me to a monitor, drew blood and attached my intravenous tube. When they finished, we sat silently listening to the sound of the baby's heartbeat. Finally I broke the silence.

"So, what happens now?" I asked.

"We've had teams out all night rounding up suspects," she answered, "I should have a full report by mid-morning." Just then, one of the men who had been standing watch over us entered and brought Nora a note. She quickly scanned it.

"Hmm…it would seem that there was an exchange of gunfire resulting in the explosion of flammable material in a building where they attempted to apprehend Marco Abruzzi and some of his associates," she said, "Early reports are that Abruzzi perished in the blaze but it'll be days before we have the forensics."

"So, what now? On to the next case?" I asked. She said nothing and I continued, "Well, it's back to the States for me."

"What do you mean?" demanded Bruce. Neither of us had heard or seen him approach, but he had overheard our conversation.

"I mean that we will apply for an annulment and I will go home," I stated, "But before I do, I would like to know everything."

Nora and Bruce exchanged glances. Finally Bruce spoke.

"Just over two years ago, my father brought Marco Abruzzi into the firm. To begin with he seemed the ideal candidate for store manager. He had connections with every corner of the world and Spenceworth's name and earnings catapulted to new heights. Father was thrilled with him and the notoriety the store was gaining under his direction. I, however, was more skeptical. There was something about him, something didn't seem quite right so I asked a friend at the agency to run a check on his background. When questionable behavior and contacts turned up, it was decided he bore watching. Enter Nora. She was assigned to the case…"

"Actually we already had Abruzzi under surveillance for quite some time," Nora broke in, "We were convinced that he had ties to an Asian smuggling ring. When he joined Spenceworth's we concluded it would just be a matter of time before he would use the store to transport stolen merchandise legitimately. We suspected that buyers of the pilfered items would be told to place bonafide orders for goods at Spenceworth's. The stolen loot was packed inside of the legitimate order and shipped off, right under everyone's nose. Of course we had a pretty good idea of what was going on but we had to let the operation continue in order to discover all the players."

"Unfortunately," Bruce resumed, "I confided in my father about the situation. He must have given Marco some reason, by word or action, to be suspicious. We believe my parents were deliberately murdered. Marco couldn't take a chance of being exposed or losing the stronghold he had in Spenceworth's. He wouldn't want to anger his Asian confederates."

"How did Jack figure into this?" I asked.

"I'm afraid I approached him and asked him to trail certain packages sent from Spenceworth's to the United States," Nora answered, "We would advise him of shipping dates and addresses. He provided surveillance for us on known members of this ring and he discovered several new ones we had not previously known about."

"So he knew you were an MI5 agent?" I asked.

"He had known for years," she replied, "He had done other work for me."

"I was the only one in the dark," I said angrily.

"He couldn't say anything to you, love," she answered, "And after what happened to Bruce's parents we clamped down. It was strictly need-to-know. After Jack and Alex were…after the accident we knew you were in danger. We had to get you nearby where we could protect you. Several of our best operatives accompanied you on the plane ride and saw you safely into my charge at Heathrow."

"So this whole business of my starting a new life was entirely premeditated. Phony job, phony marriage," I stated. Nora, and Bruce, started to protest, but I cut them short. "Please, I'm not angry, really, I'm not. For the most part, I understand why you handled things the way you did and, in some sense, I'm grateful to you both for looking out for my safety." To Bruce I said, "Now I understand what you meant about avenging our households." He looked surprised but I went on, "Yes, I was awake. Well, one can certainly say it has been exciting what with secret passages and real life spies and shoot-outs. So, what about your kidnapping? What made them pick you up?"

"Unknowingly I must have said or done something to make Lydia Markham suspicious," Bruce answered,

"She informed Marco and the rest you know. She was the mole in the executive suite. But despite Marco's, shall we say, persuasive tactics, I said nothing and kept insisting I knew nothing, although Marco was not fooled by my protestations."

"It's a miracle you weren't killed," I stated.

"Yes, well I have the bravery of two of the people I trust most in the world to thank for that," Bruce replied, "Although one of whom I should put over my knee for pulling such a stunt in her condition…"

"Yes, well," I interrupted, "Look, I realize you two have had my best interests at heart through this whole thing, even if you went to some extreme measures to protect me. However, I believe…" I started, but was cut off.

"I don't think that you should make any decisions tonight," declared Bruce, interrupting me.

"He's right, love," Nora chimed in, "You are weak and still in a state of shock. Now, I think it's time we cleared out and let you get some sleep. We will be just outside if you need anything."

"Nora…," I started.

"Goodnight," she said firmly. She left the room with Bruce in tow. He looked back at me as if he wanted to say something, but changed his mind. I had never seen him looking so dejected.

I lay back on my pillows, exhausted but allowing my mind to replay the day's events. Pictures ran through my mind and I could scarcely believe what I saw. Charles and I creeping through the sewer, Bruce's dramatic rescue, my being shot. It was like watching a movie except I was the heroine. I wondered what was next. What would I do? What should I do about my marriage? Would I remain in England? Once I had begun to believe that I might belong with the Spenceworths, but now somehow it didn't seem right. I felt as if I had been forced upon them and yet, I still sensed a strong bond with Bruce. I remained awake long into the night trying to divine the answers to my questions.

# CHAPTER NINETEEN

I CERTAINLY DIDN'T get much sleep and was sitting up when Bruce and Nora came in early the next morning.

"Leigh, darling, how are you feeling this morning?" Nora inquired in as cheerful a tone as she could muster.

"I'm fine, really," I said, "Look I..."

"Please," Bruce cut in, "Before you say anything. I cannot imagine what must be going through your mind. This whole thing has been, well, fantastic to say the least. I want to make something very clear. I was not forced to marry you. I did so because I wanted to do so. I know you are feeling uncertain about things at the moment and I would like to make a proposal. Instead of returning to the States, why not stay at Mereness Castle? No one will bother you. You can take as much time as you need to work things through and at least we'll be fairly close by should you need...or want us."

I looked from him to Nora. She sat silently and I wondered why she failed to add her two cents worth as usual. Bruce looked tired but determined. I'm not sure why I didn't just admit right then that I only wanted him to put his arms around me and hold me. I realized looking at him that I truly had feelings for him and that I really needed and wanted him. The truth was that I did not want to leave him or Nora. Put it down to stubborn, foolish pride that I did not reach out to either of them then.

"The castle?" I repeated.

"Yes," said Bruce, "Please, Leigh."

The moment was so intense. Both he and Nora were looking at me as though they too wanted to reach out, but something also held them back.

"I…yes…I think that would be a good idea," I agreed.

"Excellent!" exclaimed Bruce, "I will make the necessary arrangements."

When he had left the room Nora said, "You have made him a very happy man."

"I don't know if I can make him a happy man," I replied.

"Oh yes you can, and you will," she returned confidently, "Now Dr. Thompson is going to release you today as all is well with you and the baby. And since your wound is healing nicely he says there is no reason why you should stay. Ah, look, I would be glad to accompany you to Mereness if you'd like."

She was my tried and true friend and I knew it in my heart. "Thanks for offering Nora, but I could do with some time to myself," I answered.

"Of course, I understand," she said. Just then Bruce re-entered the room

"I've seen to everything. The helicopter will be here later today to take you directly to the castle. I've rung up Mrs. Arnold. She and Mr. Arnold will be at your disposal. Mrs. Major will send a bag round from Brookside for you…" He paused, "Well, then…"

"Bruce, what of Rob?" I asked, wondering how my sudden departure would be explained to the boy.

"I will tell him that you are going to the castle for a much needed rest and that we will…that we will be seeing you soon," he answered. "I'll just be going then…. please, ring up if there is anything…" He looked at me and swiftly departed.

"Nora…" I started.

"He'll be fine Ashleigh, don't worry," she said, "He is trying to respect your need for some time alone, we all are. Hell, it isn't as if we don't understand what a whirlwind you've been caught up in these last several months and weeks. But, love, you should know that the man truly has feelings for you. And if you don't know it, I hope you'll finally decide to give him the chance to show you. Whatever decisions you make, you know I'll stand behind you. I know Bruce will, too."

I said nothing. I did know that I needed time to clear my mind and sort through the happenings of the last several months. I planned to use the time at Mereness Castle to do just that and to make some decisions about my future.

Nora stayed by my side until the helicopter arrived later that day. It landed on the hospital roof and she insisted on seeing me off. Even after the craft took off she stood there waving. I stared after her until she was out of sight.

# CHAPTER TWENTY

IN SCOTLAND I was dropped off on the castle lawn to find Mr. and Mrs. Arnold waiting for me with the carriage. I recalled how shocked and pleasantly surprised I had been on my first visit there. Bruce had referred to the magnificent fortress as a "summer place". I couldn't imagine what Bruce must have told the Arnolds about my self-imposed retreat, but as before, Mrs. Arnold acted as if nothing was out of order. She and Mr. Arnold welcomed me with open arms, then placed me in the carriage. Mr. Arnold said my luggage would arrive later by special courier. Mrs. Arnold filled the short ride to the castle with conversation about the latest news from the village. In no time we entered the inner courtyard, disembarked and made our way indoors.

"Now, then, lass," she said, "What will ye be wantin' to do first?"

It was early evening and I was tired. "I think I'll have a bath and turn in early."

"And what about nourishment?" she asked.

"Perhaps a sandwich and a glass of milk," I suggested, "If that wouldn't be any trouble?"

"It would be my pleasure," she responded smiling, "I'll just go and draw the bath…no, I insist…and while ye soak I'll prepare the food."

"Thank you so much Mrs. Arnold," I said.

She put her arm around me and we climbed the stairs with Mr. Arnold in tow. She prepared the bath, while he assembled the luggage rack on which my bags would be placed, and then they left me. I soaked in the tub a good long time. When I dressed and re-entered the bedchamber I found the fireplace lit and my supper tray on the table near the fire. From my chair I could look out the window and view the North Sea. The sight was breathtaking and had a calming effect on me. When I had finished eating I took a pillow from the bed and propped it up behind me in the chair. Although I was anxious to begin some serious contemplation about my situation, I could not seem to focus. I sat gazing out over the sea; my mind felt numb. At some point I dozed off. I woke in the wee hours of the morning. Someone, Mrs. Arnold I guessed, had covered me with a blanket. She had probably looked in on me, found me asleep and placed the bedcover over me. I moved from the chair to the bed and went back to sleep.

When I awoke again, I found the room flooded with bright light. I glanced at the clock on the nightstand and saw that it was late morning. I rose and dressed and tidied the room. The outdoors looked so inviting that I decided to walk along the beach and then into the village. Downstairs the Arnolds were busy with chores. Mrs. Arnold helped me change the dressing on my shoulder wound and then made me a fine breakfast, insisting I should be well nourished to start the day right. After the meal I walked the beach for several miles, then doubled back and made my way into town, leisurely strolling up one street and down the next.

This became a morning ritual with me and day after day I followed the same routine. I usually talked with Nora once during the day, never Bruce. Nora said that he wanted to respect my space but she made sure to relay his heartfelt sentiments daily. She kept me informed about the goings on at Brookside and about the pertinent developments in the case. It seemed that the agency had pulled off a major coup in shutting down, or at least seriously disabling, the international smuggling ring.

Days passed, and then a fortnight. Tuesday was market day. I had planned to join the Arnolds on their trip to town, but had begged off at the last minute. I felt extraordinarily tired after my morning walk and decided to remain behind. I went to my room, placed a pillow in my favorite chair by the window and then sank down into it. Almost immediately I dozed off. Sometime later I awoke and sat up. I gasped at the sight before me. Marco Abruzzi was sitting on the bed watching me. I noticed the revolver laying in his lap.

"Why, Mrs. Spenceworth," he said coyly, "Whatever is the matter?"

I was stunned at the sight of him and surmised immediately that I was in grave danger. I was relieved about the fact that the Arnolds were safe in town. They would not be back for several hours and I prayed that whatever the ordeal was to be, it would be over by the time they returned. Marco looked like he hadn't slept in days, and there was a murderous desperation behind his eyes.

"Get up!" he commanded. I was so horrified at the sight of him I sat motionless. "On your feet, bitch!" he ordered again only this time he rose and came over to me, dragging me to my feet by my hair.

"Oh…Marco…please," I pleaded.

"Move!" he said as he shoved the revolver in my back and forced me out of the room, down the hall and up a winding staircase. I guessed he must have visited the fortress at some time previously as he clearly knew his way around. Eventually we found ourselves out on the roof.

"I can't think of a more perfect ending for you, my dear," he laughed, "The grieving widow jumps to her death after losing a second husband and child."

"Oh my God, what have you done?" I shrieked.

"I've just come from Brookside," he said deliberately, "Where I am sure by now, someone has discovered the bodies," he finished laughing and glancing at his watch.

His words stung my brain. I lunged at him but was no match for him. He easily subdued me and then shoved me roughly.

"Start walking…no not that way, seaside. I want them to find you on the rocks below," he laughed wildly.

I walked a few paces and then turned around and stopped, "Marco…"

"Shut up and get moving!" he said angrily.

"I need to know about Bruce and Rob," I begged sobbing.

He pointed the revolver at me and began advancing toward me. "Move or so help me I'll…"

He broke off abruptly, stopping dead in his tracks. A look of sheer terror had spread across his face. He was no longer looking at me, but rather, beyond and behind me. I turned around to follow his gaze. Hovering quite close to us was Robyn Spenceworth. This sighting of her was contrary to the ones I had previously been privy to. She was not smiling and inviting us to follow her. She was enraged and advancing in our direction. As I stood immobilized, she passed me heading straight for Marco. He had begun retreating backwards, open-mouthed, never taking his eyes from her. He went over the edge without a sound. When she turned back toward me, she was smiling like I'd seen her do many times before and then she was gone.

Just then I became aware of a helicopter that had come dangerously close to the roof. As it hovered in the air a door flew open and I saw someone jump onto the roof. All at once I realized it was Bruce and he was running toward me. The sight of him revived me and I raced toward him. Within seconds we were holding each other, crying.

"Please take me home and never let me go!" I requested, sobbing.

"Never!" he promised, holding me tighter.

# EPILOGUE

The weeks and months following Marco's death were filled with revelations. Marco had survived the fire and spent days in hiding planning his revenge. Apparently he had stopped at Brookside before coming to the castle, but upon learning from one of the gardeners that the family was not at home headed straight for the castle. He must have expected to find us all there but when there was only me, he tormented me into believing he had done away with my family, again.

Bruce told me that Elizabeth Major had come to him that fateful day insisting that I was in danger (I learned from Mrs. Major that Robyn had 'alerted' her to my predicament). Bruce said he had never seen Mrs. Major so agitated and at once sent for the helicopter and agency backup. As we had stood embracing on the roof we heard the sound of several cars arriving. Hand in hand we peered over the edge to see Nora and several agents race from their cars. Nora had knelt beside Marco and then looked up at us shaking her head. By the time the body was removed and my statement taken, it had been too late to return to Brookside. Our group stayed the night at the castle. Bruce and I spent that night together in the bridal suite, as man and wife.

We returned home the following day and were reunited with Rob and Charles and Mrs. Major. I felt as if that day were the first day of the rest of my life. It was glorious to be reunited with loved ones and relieving to know that the dark cloud that had hung over both our houses had finally been lifted. There was no longer a sense of danger in the air, but rather a sense of quiet excitement.

Although Nora said the case against the smuggling ring had not come to a close, we wrapped up our roles by giving our statements, being debriefed and being sworn to secrecy. Bruce and I were not allowed to speak about anything we had seen or heard, and Bruce's role as the 'Creeper' was to remain confidential. Nora advised us that a story indicating that the mysterious robber had moved on would be leaked to the press. She also said that an anonymous donation would be made by the agency to Lloyds of London, the insurance carrier for most of the stolen articles, to cover premiums paid out as a result of the thefts.

I asked Bruce what it felt like to play the role of the bold robber. He took some time before answering but admitted the job had been exhilarating, in a nerve-wracking sort of way. He had been supplied with a device that deciphered a safe's combination within seconds, therefore enabling him to complete the thefts rapidly. I learned that Charles had been his accomplice. Of course he had no prior experience in the intelligence world but when Bruce had confided the problem at hand and subsequent mission plan, Charles being ever loyal to the family offered his assistance.

And as it turned out, Charles' relationship with the servants of several households had proved invaluable. His vicarious knowledge of a family's comings and goings and proposed holidays allowed Bruce to plan his robberies. Donald and Hugh had been servants but had been sacked several months earlier due to economic changes in the houses where they worked. They had lost their homes, forcing their families into impoverished living conditions. Charles had kept in touch with them, bringing them news of potential work, food and clothing. Bruce and Charles made a special trip back to see them and to thank them for their generous help in our hour of need. Bruce offered the men jobs at Spenceworth's, which they gladly accepted, giving them a chance to get back on their feet.

I spent many afternoons in the gardens behind the house hoping to see Robyn. I owed her mine and my baby's life. But I never saw her again. Mrs. Major believed it was because she no longer had a reason to watch over us. Her family was safe and happy once more. She had obviously been a remarkable woman in life, and I felt so honored to have been privy to the brief encounters I shared with her. I often wondered, however, why she had chosen to appear to me rather than to Bruce. I reasoned it was probably because I could maintain objectivity while Bruce would most likely have become highly emotional at the sight of her. I decided the time was not yet right to tell him about my experience with her. One day he suggested moving her portrait, perhaps as a gesture of sensitivity for my feelings. I immediately rejected the idea, insisting that she remain just where she was. I tried to explain that it was important for her to be there, watching over her family. Bruce honored my wishes, but was clearly confused at my motives.

He returned to work at Spenceworth's and I spent my days getting better acquainted with friends and neighbors, helping Rob with his schoolwork and writing several articles about the store and the import-export business in general. From time to time Bruce and I would assist Nora with one of her investigations, mostly by doing paper research – no field work. She would provide us with reams of papers that needed sifting through and we would provide her with a summary and analysis. Bruce and I sat up many a night working together. Our relationship became stronger and deeper during those days, and I realized that Nora had indeed been right about the fact that we belonged together.

Nora and I began having boxes shipped from storage in the United States and together we sorted through them. Many of Jack's and Alex's possessions I repacked and stored in the attic. Some things I decided to donate to charity and others I gave to Bruce and Rob. Although seeing and touching their belongings was still painful, it was a process I needed to complete to help me heal. I was blessed to have a second chance with another family, but my love for my first husband and child would remain eternal.

Jacklyn Grant Spenceworth was born as the sun rose on Valentine's Day. She came so quickly that Bruce, assisted by Mrs. Major, actually delivered her before Dr. Thompson could arrive. Bruce had been calm under pressure but once the doctor appeared, he wearily sank down into a chair. Rob and Charles had come in to see the baby and afterward Rob stood next to his father, patting his back. As I surveyed the room full of people and my newest gift from God, I realized that He had given me a tremendous opportunity for a second chance. I intended to make every moment count.

Days after Jacklyn was born, family and friends assembled in the little chapel behind the house for her christening. Before the ceremony, as we were talking with Father Walsh, he predicted we would be gathered around the altar again, next time welcoming twins into God's family. Bruce and I smiled, elated by the priest's premonition.

After the ceremony our group made its way back to the house for Jacklyn's party. As I left the chapel I looked up to heaven and offered a silent prayer of thanks for sunrises and new beginnings.